LOVE AND VALOR

BY ROSELLE ZUBEY

To the memory of
James Horner
1953 – 2015

LOVE
AND
VALOR

by Roselle Zubey

Copyright © 2021
Roselle Zubey

Library of Congress Control Number 020924983

ISBN 13: 978-1-63752-446-6

All rights reserved. No part of this book may be reproduced or transmitted in any form or by any means, electronic or mechanical, including photocopying, recording, or by any information storage and retrieval system, without permission in writing from the copyright owner.

This book was manufactured in the United States of America

Basket Road Press
Philadelphia, PA ● Harrisburg, PA
USA

First Edition

To order additional books contact:
info@basketroadpress.com

PROLOGUE

1964

Susannah Allen Hughes was exhausted. Ever since her parents had died she had been working on a book about their experiences in World War One. Both her parents, James and Mary, had passed away a week apart, so she was writing this book as a tribute to them and the pioneering lives they led during the Great War.

While Susannah was working on her book, her older sister, Jenny, was uncertain about trying to talk to her. Jenny knew that *Love and Valor* was going to be important. It seemed everything Susannah did was important. Jenny admired Susannah's career as a historian. She was always doing something interesting. On that note, Jenny decided to go downstairs and see if Susannah needed her help.

Susannah was taking a small break and was surprised when she heard a knock on her door.

"Come in," Susannah said.

Jenny came into their father's study. "I came to see how things are going for you," Jenny said.

"They're going well," Susannah said. "Your going through the attic was a stupendous help for me. I credit you with being my research assistant in the acknowledgments."

"Thank you," Jenny said. "That makes me feel better."

When Jenny fell silent, Susannah could see that something was wrong.

"What's going on?" Susannah asked her sister.

"Sometimes I don't feel like I'm doing enough to honor Mother and Father or follow in their footsteps," Jenny said. "You and Matthew have your pilot's licenses. I didn't get one."

"Hold on," Susannah said. "You became a surgeon, Jen. You followed in Mother's footsteps brilliantly. Father always understood about you not getting your pilot's license because he knew you were undertaking a difficult study. He loved you very much and was proud of you."

"How do you know this?" Jenny asked.

"I read his diaries," Susannah said. "Would you like to read them?"

"I think I would," Jenny said. "It might help me feel better."

Susannah went through the materials on her desk until she found her father's diaries. She picked up a box and piled them in.

"I'm going to go upstairs and read these," Jenny said. "Thank you so much for lending them to me."

"You're so welcome," Susannah said. "I love you and want to help you if I can."

As soon as Jenny went out, Susannah went back to work.

A little later, Susannah decided to take another break from her editing and find her husband, Anthony. Anthony was working on a project of his own, restoring a biplane that her father had designed when he was at Cambridge University. She went to Jenny's room to see if she wanted to go along.

Jenny was still busy reading the diaries when Susannah stuck her head in the door.

"I'm going out to the airfield to find Anthony," Susannah said. "Would you like to come along?"

"I'd love to," Jenny said.

She carefully marked her place in the diary and followed Susannah out.

"Thank you for including me," Jenny said on the way to the airfield. "I'm anxious to see Father's aeroplane."

"This is a family project," Susannah said. "Please don't forget that you're a part of the family."

"I won't," Jenny said.

When Jenny and Susannah got to the airfield, Susannah saw Anthony hard at work making her father's aeroplane flyable again. Anthony smiled when he looked up and saw Susannah and Jenny. He walked over to his wife and gave her a kiss. Then he gave his sister-in-law a hug.

"How's the book coming?" Anthony asked his wife. "I thought you'd still be hard at work."

"I needed a break," Susannah said. "I'm about finished, though. I'm wondering how Father and Mother survived that madness. I brought Jenny along to see the aeroplane."

"I think their love for each other kept them strong," Anthony said.

"I think you're right." Susannah ran her hand over the new fabric that had helped restore her father's aeroplane. She smiled when Jenny hesitated to do the same.

"You can touch it," Susannah said. "It's fabric coated with a varnish called dope."

Jenny smiled when she touched the aeroplane. She felt as though her father was smiling down on her from heaven.

"Father designed this?" she asked.

"Yes he did while he was at university," Susannah said.

"I feel close to Father right now," Jenny said.

"So do I," Susannah said. "If I get to fly her when she's finished, would you like a ride?"

"That would be fun," Jenny said. "Thank you."

Susannah hoped she would get to fly the aeroplane when she was finished. She was looking forward to flying her, in fact. She had kept up a pilot's certificate from the time she was eighteen years old. Flying was very much in the Allen family blood. But for now Susannah knew that she had to do everything she could to finish her book.

PART ONE

VALOR

1918

James Allen wondered what exactly was going on. The war was in its fourth year. But he was still uncertain about what he and his men were supposed to be doing. James and the pilots under his command went from simple reconnaissance missions to mapping the entire German front including behind their lines. Their artillery observation controlled the guns and raised hell with their targets. James looked at the paperwork he had to do. It was the worst part of his job as a flight commander in the Royal Flying Corps, so he decided to get it over with as soon as he could. He wished that Baker, the office sergeant, was there to help him. But he wasn't. James was done within the hour and went to the officer's mess to spend time with his men.

He saw that Robin Milne was playing pool with Michael Warner, one of the observers went to watch them play. The men both stood to attention. "Stand easy," James said. "Finish your game."

Warner sank an easy shot, leaving Milne in a bind about what to do next. Milne's best shot would be a difficult one. He studied the board and finally took his shot.

"Good shot, Milne," James said when the young pilot succeeded. "You almost have him."

James watched closely as Warner took a shot and missed. Milne stood ready to take his turn and sank the last shot to win the game.

"Good game," Warner said as he shook hands with the younger man.

Milne turned to face James. James guided the younger man over the sofa and sat with him to talk.

"How do you feel about going to Home Establishment?" James asked.

"I want to stay in the action, sir," Milne said. "My score is not that impressive."

"But you did become an ace," James said. "That is quite an accomplishment. You shouldn't compare yourself to other pilots. That can only get you killed. You have to concentrate on your own score and situation."

"You're right, sir," Milne said. "I think I did it because of my family's expectations of me. They wanted me to enlist in the cavalry as my father had done during the Boer War. They were dismayed when I chose to become a pilot instead."

"I know you love and respect your family," James said. "But we're under enough pressure as it is. We don't need any more."

"Understood, sir," Milne said. "And thank you."

James stood and faced Milne. He hoped the younger man couldn't read the concern in his eyes. "Don't you have a reconnaissance flight soon?" James asked.

"I do, sir," Milne said.

"I'll come with you," James said.

"Yes, sir," Milne said.

James returned to his office to get into his flying coat, scarf, and other gear. He wasn't sure why he felt he should go with Milne. He knew that the young man had proved himself to be quite a capable pilot time and again. James just knew for certain that he had to go with him.

James went out to the hangar to check on his aeroplane while he was waiting for Milne. He trusted his mechanics implicitly. But he felt safer knowing that he had checked his aeroplane himself. It was an old habit that had sprung from his background as an engineer.

As he finished, Milne came to join him. He didn't say anything to James because he was intent on the mission ahead. Milne's observer, Steven Parker, joined him. James waited for his observer, Michael Warner. When Warner came out, James climbed into his cockpit while Warner climbed into his.

Jones stood in front of James's aeroplane. He had a hold of the propeller.

"Switch off, petrol on," Jones said.

"Switch off, petrol on," James said, repeating the mechanic's instruction as he carried it out.

"Air closed. Suck in," Jones said.

"Air closed. Suck in," James said.

"Contact," Jones said.

"Contact," James said.

Jones pulled down on the propeller, and the engine came roaring to life. James made a signal with his hands. The mechanics pulled away the blocks that were holding the aeroplane still. Then James taxied down the field and rose into the sky. Milne followed not too far behind him.

As they made their way to the area they were supposed to photograph, James kept a close eye on Milne. He was afraid that something bad was going to happen. James couldn't allow anything to happen to the younger man because Milne was going home.

When they arrived on site, Warner took out his camera and began to shoot. While James and Milne were carrying out their mission, James kept his eyes open and Warner took aerial photographs of the targets the artillery was going to attack. Just then James saw two German aeroplanes coming out of the sun. He wondered if Milne saw it. When he saw Milne looking in his direction, James wiggled his wings to signal an attack. Milne followed James to the attack, but Milne knew he was in trouble.

Warner made quick work of their German opponent, but James quickly saw that Milne and Parker were in trouble with theirs. Before he could get there, James saw black smoke coming out of Milne's aeroplane. He felt rage like never before as he went after the German who had shot Milne down. He looked around to find the younger pilot. James saw that Milne was still going downward with smoke coming out of his tail. When Milne tried to land, it crashed into a heap and burst into flames.

After James landed, he ran to find that Milne was on the ground and not moving. Parker lay a bit farther away. He was also lying still. Warner went to check on Parker, while James checked on Milne. Fortunately, they were behind the British lines so they were safe.

"Sir, I can't feel my legs," Milne said when he came around. "I'm scared."

"I'm right here," James said. "Warner and I won't leave until I'm sure you're alright:"

James saw Warner coming toward him. He didn't like the sad look on the observer's face.

"Parker didn't make it, sir," Warner said.

"Damn it," James said. "When will this end?"

Then James and Warner saw that men were approaching. James said a prayer that they were Allied troops. When they got closer James was relieved to see that the men were British.

"Be careful when you lift him," James said. "I think his back might be broken because he can't feel his legs. There's another man a little way off. But he's already dead."

"Understood, sir," one of the medics said. The medics were gentle when they lifted Milne onto the stretcher. Then all of a sudden there was more artillery fire coming down on them. James and Warner ran toward their aeroplane. James prayed that they would be able to take off under fire. Before they went their separate ways, James put a hand on Milne's shoulder and gave it a gentle squeeze.

"I'll find you," James said. "Just concentrate on getting better."

"I will, sir," Milne said. "Thank you."

James watched as the other men took Milne away. Then he continued toward his aeroplane. He made sure that Warner was keeping up with him. When they got to their aeroplane, James jumped into the pilot's cockpit. Warner stood in front waiting to turn the propeller. When he saw that James was ready, Warner gave the propeller a spin. The engine started on the first try, and Warner jumped in. James taxied under heavy fire and let out a breath when he and Warner finally rose into the air.

Flying home James realized that losing men was hard, especially men like Milne, who had grown as a pilot and as a man while he was under his command. Parker had been one of his best observers, too. Encouraging his men was always James's style. It didn't even cross his mind that he was a duke. All James wanted to be was Captain James Allen, flight commander of C Flight in the Royal Flying Corps. James knew that made all the difference for him and his men. He thought of his men not just as brother officers but as brothers.

By the time he got back, the rest of James's men were worried about him and Warner because they were three hours overdue. They were relieved to see them come through the door but were surprised to see that they were alone.

"What happened, sir?" Corky Robinson, the lone American pilot, asked James.

"Milne got shot down," James said. "Fortunately, we were behind our lines when it happened. We stayed with him until help came."

James went right to the bar and got himself a stiff drink. Then he sat alone on the sofa. Sean McElroy came and sat with James to listen if he needed to talk.

"I don't like it when I lose men," James finally said. "I feel as though I failed in my duty as a flight commander because it's part of my job to keep all of you safe."

"The fact that you try so hard to keep us alive means a lot to all of us, sir" McElroy said.

"You prevented the Boche aeroplane from taking more shots and killing Milne. You risked your life and quite possibly saved Milne's."

"How did I save Milne?" James asked. "He has a broken back. He may be paralyzed for life. Steven Parker is dead."

"The fact is that Milne is still alive, sir," McElroy said. "With all due respect you should think about that."

James took a big drink out of his glass as he thought about what McElroy said. It didn't take him long to realize that McElroy was right.

"If I may say so, sir, you're being hard on yourself," McElroy said to James. "We need you to stay with us if we're going to make it through this hell alive."

All James could do was look at McElroy. James hoped that McElroy would beat the odds and stay alive himself because James needed him to play his beautiful music to get through this war with his sanity intact.

"I'm going to try to get some rest," James said. "I'll be down for supper."

As James started up the stairs to his quarters, he heard McElroy play beautiful music on the piano. That was what got James through time and time again. Well, it was that beautiful music and thinking of his sweetheart Mary Gordon that got him through.

But James knew he couldn't sleep or appreciate the music or think of Mary Gordon right then. He had to write that damn condolence letter to Steven Parker's wife. James knew that he shouldn't feel that way. It was just that those letters were hard for him to write.

He sat at his desk for a moment. Then James got out his stationery and pen and began to write.

Dear Mrs. Parker—I am writing to express my deep condolences to you on the death of your husband, Steven. I truly admired his wonderful humor and his great talent as an observer. That talent made him the best observer and highly valued member of my flight. Even if that weren't the case, I would still say, as I said above, that I am sorry for your loss. Please accept my deepest sympathy.

Sincerely yours,
Captain James Allen
Flight Commander, C Flight
Royal Flying Corps

The day of Parker's funeral, the sun was blazing hot. The men of C Flight gathered together for his burial. James only watched as the pallbearers gathered and Parker's body was wrapped in cloth. James hadn't forgotten how Parker's body felt cold and rigid when he laid a hand on it and said a prayer.

"Do you need a hand, sir?" Corky Robinson asked.

"No, thank you, Robinson," James said. "Just keep up with the rest of the men."

"Yes, sir," Corky Robinson said as he ran off to join the others.

While he was walking to the cemetery at the top of the hill, James wondered again how long the killing would go on. For a moment he questioned a God who would allow carnage like this to happen. But then he remembered there were often times when God did things for no reason or left the reason unknown. James remembered his Sunday school teachers saying God was mysterious. But he knew deep down that without his faith he would have cracked a long time ago. Finally he reached the cemetery and stood with the rest of his men.

James and the men watched the padre as he read the burial service. But no one could hear what he said. The gloom ran deep. Sean McElroy stood next to James to give him what comfort he could. While the padre spoke, McElroy wondered when it would be his turn to die. He put his hand gently on James's arm and gave it a squeeze. James nodded his thanks.

When the burial service was over, James, Sean McElroy, Corky Robinson, and the rest of the men threw dirt into Steven Parker's grave. Before the grave was filled in, James, McElroy, and Corky Robinson led the rest of the men as they walked away.

Back at the officer's mess, the men of C Flight realized it was lunchtime. When they sat down to eat all the men, especially James, noticed the two empty chairs at the table. In that moment James couldn't help but to feel relief that Robin Milne had survived. That was the one blessing in this horrific and tragic situation.

Later, when the day's missions were complete, James was still devastated about Steven Parker's funeral. He decided to write a letter to Mary. He sat at his desk and took out his Royal Flying Corps stationery and a pen. He wrote as quickly as he could for fear that his heart would break all over again.

Dear Mary, love—I'm writing another letter so soon because I need to talk to someone about what happened today. Nothing bad happened to me except that I was devastated by Steven Parker's funeral. Parker was the best observer on the flight and a consummate jokester. You think I would be hardened to funerals by now. I've been in the Royal Flying Corps for six years and have seen so many terrible crashes. He was thirty-two years old. So he had a lot of experience. It doesn't make any damn sense to me. At the same time, I'm so glad you're in my life, Mary. I have to say that. I truly believe that my depth of love for you and my wanting to get home to you so we can have our life together at last is keeping me alive. I love you with all my heart and soul.

James

The reason James wrote to Mary was because she was a doctor and knew about terrible losses. Mary was the chief medical officer and a surgeon at the Abbaye de Ste. Marie field hospital. She had lost her entire family in different ways. Her first husband was brutally murdered. She had seen thousands of horribly maimed and wounded men come through Ste. Marie in the four years of the war. Mary knew the horror of war better than anyone on the outside could. He missed Mary more than he could put words to. James so wished the war would end soon so he could go home and marry her. His father had died so there was nothing now that stood in their way. James had never understood why his father had opposed the marriage because Mary was a woman doctor. He should have gone through with marrying Mary anyway. James didn't care about the title at all. He was only the duke of Essex now because his older brother, Matthew, had died—well that and the fact that he was too much of a coward to stand up to his father. All he cared about was being an engineer and pilot and serving his country. As James thought of Mary, he knew that all the problems with his father were now in the past. James had to concentrate on staying alive so he could get home and marry his great love. When James finished the letter, he read it to himself, put it in an envelope, and sealed it closed. He would put it in the next mail out. James lay down on his bed and fell into a deep sleep.

In the meanwhile, Mary was looking at an X-ray of Robin Milne's back. She could see where the fragments of bone were. Fortunately there did not seem to be any damage to his spine. He would need major rehabilitation, but it was certain that he would walk again. Mary got ready to perform the surgery.

In the operating room, Mary's concentration was intense. She did not want to harm Milne through any mistake that she would make. A nurse saw that Mary was perspiring, so she wiped Mary's head with her towel. Finally the job was done. Mary stitched the incision closed and breathed a sigh of relief. She took off her surgical garb then went to her office.

Mary picked up her phone and dialed. She hoped against hope that she could get through to James's flight. She urgently wanted to let James know that Robin Milne was safe and under her care.

"C Flight," Baker said.

"Is Captain Allen available, please?" Mary asked.

"I'm sorry but he's out on a mission right now," Baker said. "May I take a message?"

"Yes," Mary said. "My name is Dr. Mary Gordon. I'm the chief medical officer at the Abbaye de Ste. Marie field hospital. I wanted to let Captain Allen know that Robin Milne is a patient here and under my care."

"Thank you for letting us know," Baker said. "Captain Allen will appreciate that."

"It was my pleasure," Mary said.

Baker wrote down what she said and left the paper on James's desk.

Mary went to her quarters to try and rest. She didn't know how long this lull would last, so she decided to take advantage of the situation.

But Mary didn't have much chance to relax because she saw an envelope on her dresser. Her hands started to shake when she saw the letter was from James.

She carefully opened the envelope and read the letter slowly. Tears came to her eyes. When she finished, Mary put the letter back in the envelope. She got out her stationery and began to write.

Darling James—I am so grateful to God that I finally got a letter from you. I'm sorry about Steven Parker. I know that it's hard for you to lose men. That is the horrific and unfortunate side of war. I'm so tired of seeing handsome young men with so much to give torn to pieces. All I can suggest you do is pray. I do that all the time for the young men who come through Ste. Marie, especially the pilots. I always think of you when I treat a horribly injured pilot. To be honest I wonder if the next patient I see will be you. That frightens me more than coming under fire from German aeroplanes. Please don't hesitate to write to me or, better still, come to see me. We have to stick together as best we can, my love. I am close by. But because I can't be with you all the time as I would wish, it feels like I'm miles away. As I said above, I am so sorry about Steven Parker. I know how much you care about your men. Even though that caring may be difficult, I still admire you very much for that. It also hurts my heart that I can't be there by your side to help you and comfort you. I don't know if you got my message. Robin Milne is here at Ste. Marie under my care. He is doing well. I will do my best to keep writing to you. I love you more than these mere words can say. Please do be careful. Until we meet again.

Mary

The next morning James came downstairs and went into the flight office. As he opened the door, he wondered what was waiting for his men and him.

"There's new orders for you and the men, sir," Baker said.

Baker handed the paper to James. The orders were to take his flight out on another reconnaissance mission. James did not say or do anything. He was still tired even though he had had a good sleep.

"Gather the men together, please," James said.

"Yes, sir," the sergeant said.

Baker left. Soon the men gathered in the flight office.

"Quiet, please," James said.

James sat at his desk and picked up the paper that contained their orders.

"Our new assignment is to go over the German lines to observe the German artillery," James said. "It's the same kind of mission that we've always gone on, so I don't have to tell you that it's risky. I need all of you to stay alert and not do anything crazy or stupid."

James looked over his men. He hoped that he could keep them alive to fight another day. That responsibility wore heavily on his shoulders. But James knew he had to bear it as best he could.

"We have to leave straightaway," James said. "So go now and get ready."

After the men went out, James walked to the door. He took down his flying coat and scarf and got dressed. Then he decided to go to the hangar and check his aeroplane again.

He noticed streamers tied to his struts. They meant that he was the leader of the mission. He also noticed that Sean McElroy was to be his deputy. Again, being the leader was something that he took seriously. He didn't say anything to Warner when the observer joined him. James finished the checkup of his aeroplane then got in the pilot's cockpit. Once Warner got into the observer's cockpit, James checked over the instrumentation—what of it there was. When that was all finished James watched as the rest of his men got into their own aeroplanes. When they were ready, the mechanics took each pilot through the start-up procedure. James could almost go through the procedure himself from memory because he had been through it so many times in the years he was in the Royal Flying Corps.

"Switch off. Petrol on," Jones, the mechanic said.

"Switch off. Petrol on," James repeated while he was carrying out the action.

"Air closed. Suck in," Jones said.

"Air closed. Suck in," James said.

"Contact," Jones said.

"Contact," James said.

When Jones spun the propeller, the engine in James's aeroplane roared to life. He listened as the other mechanics took the men through the procedure. Then they all took off one at a time. While they were in the air, James looked carefully for the German scouts because he knew that they were going to try to stop them from crossing their lines. But James was determined to do just that. He had to uncover what the Germans were up to. James and his men had to get the proper information to help the commanders to know where and when an attack was going to take place. He would report everything he saw. He knew that Warner was busily taking photographs. So, James let him do his work. When James got back from his mission, he was exhausted. But he still had to write his report. He knew that his men were doing the same thing. While he was writing Baker came in. James decided to vent his frustration on the flight office sergeant.

"There were no signs of an attack in the offing," James said when Baker asked him how the mission went. "There was no construction. There were no signs of German troops. Nothing."

"But you and the men still have to be vigilant, sir," Baker said.

"I know that, Baker," James said. "I just wonder what the Boche are up to."

"There's no way of knowing without reconnaissance," Baker said. "But there's a letter on your desk that might lift your mood a bit, sir."

James sat at his desk and looked from Baker to the envelope. He was so glad that he got a letter from Mary. She must be magical because a letter always arrived from her when he needed it the most. James carefully opened the envelope and took the letter out.

Dearest James—There is a little break in our action, so I thought I would write and let you know that I'm still alright. I've been worried about you since the day of Steven Parker's funeral. I wonder how long this war will go on. You know that I am a strong woman. But I am near to the breaking point myself. I can understand if you are because I know that one little mistake can send you to your death. I still wish I could see you more often. I'm sorry if I'm burdening you. I know you have great responsibilities as a flight commander. But I need to talk to you through these letters as often as I can. I'm sorry this letter is so short. But I'm needed for more surgery. Know that I love you very much.

Mary

When James finished reading Mary's letter, he knew Baker had been right to say that a letter from her would lift his mood. James felt bad that there were times, like now, when he forgot that she was close by.

Once again James said a prayer that he would survive the war so he could get home to Mary and marry her. He believed in that moment that the hope of fulfilling that wish was what was keeping him alive. He carefully put Mary's letter in his pocket and took it with him when he went to join his men in the mess.

James saw that Sean McElroy and Bryan Murray, the observer who replaced Steven Parker, were playing a rowdy game of ping pong.

"I'll play the winner," James said. It took a while for there to be a winner because McElroy and Murray were so evenly matched. Finally Murray prevailed. McElroy handed his paddle to James then shook Murray's hand.

"You have to watch that one, sir," McElroy said. "He is a beast."

"Thank you for the warning, Mr. McElroy," James said. "I think I can handle him all the same."

"We'll play a point for first serve, sir," Murray said.

"Very well," James said. "Let's go."

James and Murray played an evenly matched point. Finally James prevailed and got first serve. As the game progressed, James wore Murray down. He won the game in a shutout. "Good game, sir," Murray said as he reached across to shake James's hand. "I enjoyed the challenge. Thank you."

"I did as well, Murray" James said. "Thank you, too."

James went to the bar to get a quick drink then went to his quarters to write an answer to Mary's heartfelt letter. In the privacy of his quarters, he took out his stationery and began to write.

Dearest Mary—I was overjoyed to receive your letter. I'm so glad that you're alright. I always worry about you and get angry if I hear that a hospital has been attacked. I always thought the Red Cross means you're not to be attacked. I'm still upset about Steven Parker. But, with the help of the rest of my men and with your help, I'm slowly recovering. I wonder, too, how long the war will go on. It seems like there is no end. It's true that one mistake can send me to my death. That's why I try to live each day to the fullest. I wish I could see you more often, too. But I take great consolation in your letters. You are not burdening me in any way through your letters. We are doing what people who love each other do. And I do love you very much.

James

The next day James gave the other pilots a warning. He hoped they paid attention to it because it could mean the difference between life and death.

"When we're up today, you have to pay attention to what you're doing," he said. "Even though the Germans were nowhere to be found yesterday, that doesn't mean they're not up to something. We need to find out exactly what's going on. We need to stay close together in formation so at least some of us can get back and make our reports. Is that clear?"

"Yes, sir," the men all said together.

Then they all made ready to go out on their mission. While he and Warner were sitting in their aeroplane waiting to take off, James said a prayer that he could lead all his men back home safely.

Mary was exhausted. She slowly made her way through the wards checking on the patients of Ste. Marie. Fortunately the nurses did a good job of caring for the men, so there was little that she had to do.

Still, Mary was most anxious to check on Robin Milne. She wanted to see how he was doing since she performed the surgery on his back. Finally she got to Milne's bed.

"Good morning, Lieutenant," she said to Milne.

"Good morning, Dr. Gordon," Milne said.

"How are you feeling?" Mary asked.

"As well as can be expected," Milne said. Mary absentmindedly put her hand on the back of Milne's leg.

"Dr. Gordon, can you please do that again?" Milne asked.

Mary did as Milne asked.

"What's going on, Milne?" Mary asked. "I thought I felt your hand on my leg," Milne said.

"That's good news," Mary said. "See if you can feel this." Mary put her hand on different parts of Milne's leg. She watched him to try to determine what was going on. If he was getting feeling back in his legs, that would mean that he would definitely be able to walk again.

"I felt your hand every time," Milne said.

"That's a good sign," Mary said. "That means you're starting to heal and that you'll be able to walk again. I have to check your incision now."

Mary lifted the blanket on Milne's bed "It will be two or three more days until the stitches come out,"

Mary said. "Then you'll be able to lie on your back like normal."

"Thank you for everything," Milne said.

"You're most welcome," Mary said.

When she got back to her office, Mary slumped onto her chair. She said a prayer of thanks that Milne was on the mend. Then she said a heartfelt prayer that James would survive to come back to her.

As they flew over the same area they did yesterday, James and his men found all the signs that the Germans were planning a major offensive. Railways and sidings were being constructed. The roads were being improved. There were massive munitions dumps to be seen. There were also signs of German forces massing, new airdromes, camps, and gun battery positions. James knew that he and his men would have to interfere with this preparation. They would have to cooperate with the artillery. There would have to be intensive bombing attacks. They would have to inflict casualties on the Germans and disturb their rest. They would have to take their place with the infantry on the front line. James flew slowly so Warner could take pictures that would be sent to headquarters.

When they got back to base, James and his men were silent. They had done their mission well and taken the Germans totally by surprise. They had interfered with the preparations and then some. They were all silent because they were all exhausted. Even so, there were still other missions that needed to be carried out.

"Do you think we'll be given the order to fly low over the trenches, sir?" McElroy asked.

"We probably will be," James said. "We have to be prepared for it."

When James went to the flight office, he found that there was a message for him from Mary. She told him that Robin Milne was doing well, that he was getting feeling back in his legs and would be able to walk again. James was glad that he had written to Mary about his men in his letters. That was the way she knew who Robin Milne was and that it was important that he know how Milne was doing. Even though he didn't like hospitals very much since his sister, Sara, had died, James decided to go to see Milne straightaway.

Mary was standing by the desk when James arrived at the Abbaye de Ste. Marie field hospital. He gave her a kiss on the cheek.

"I'm so glad to see you," Mary said to James. "I miss you very much even though you're close by."

"I miss you too," James said. "Can we talk after I'm done with my visit with Milne?"

"Of course we can," Mary said. "My shift doesn't start until later. We can go out in the garden where we'll have some privacy."

Without saying much of anything, Mary led James to where Milne was resting in bed. What James didn't know was that Mary was wondering if the next wounded pilot brought in would be him. It was something they rarely talked about.

"I'll leave you two to talk," she said as she put her hand on James's arm. "You can have one of the nurses find me when you're finished."

"Thank you for coming, sir," Milne said when James gently laid his hand on his shoulder.

"How are you feeling?" James asked.

"I'm glad to be alive, sir," Milne said. "Dr. Gordon said she thought there was no damage to my spine, so the paralysis will be temporary. I'll have to walk with a cane, but I will be able to walk."

"It's good to hear that," James said. "I was worried about you."

"Thank you for that, sir," Milne said.

"I would like for us to keep in touch," James said. "I will contact my solicitor and make provision for you in case you need anything. My daughter is already provided for, so you must not hesitate to contact him. I know you have to take care of your mother."

James saw the notepad on the table next to Milne's bed. He picked it up and wrote his London address and his solicitor's address on it. Then he put the notepad back on the table.

"That means a lot, sir," Milne said. "I kept in touch with my father's publishers. They want me to start writing children's books where my father left off. But that will take some time now. I have an idea of writing a story about a pilot and his lady doctor sweetheart. If it's alright with you, I want to base it on you and Dr. Gordon."

"That would be fine," James said. "I feel honored by that. I'm sure Mary will too."

"Feel honored by what?" Mary asked as she walked up.

"I want to write a children's book and have the main characters be based on you and Captain Allen, Dr. Gordon," Milne said.

"You're right. That would be an honor," Mary said. "Even though it's a children's book, I'm anxious to read it now."

"Thank you," Milne said.

"I have to be going," James said. "Please take care of yourself and let me know how you are."

Milne reached out and James gave his hand a hearty shake. Then James and Mary walked off together. James felt deeply moved by the good care that Mary and her nurses had given to Milne.

"Thank you for all that you've done for Milne," he said. "I'm so glad and relieved that he won't be paralyzed for life."

"There's no need for thanks, James," Mary said. "It's what I was born to do. I'm glad I had the skills to help him."

When James and Mary went out into the garden, they sat on one of the benches. Mary took hold of James's hand when she saw how sad he looked. James held onto her hand as if for dear life.

"I'm worried about you," Mary said. "You look so sad. Can you tell me what's going on?"

"I don't think I should be going into detail," James said. "All I can say is that we might be getting orders for a mission that is dangerous."

"But you haven't gotten them yet?" Mary asked.

James shook his head no.

"I regret that I didn't stand up to my father when he forbade us to marry," James said. "There are times when I wish Jenny was your daughter instead of Elizabeth's."

Mary didn't know what she could do to help James. That upset her. She took hold of his hands and held on tight.

"What can I do to help you?" she finally asked James with tears in her eyes.

"You're helping me by sitting here with me," James said. "I know you don't need the money, but I want you to know that before I came over here four years ago, I made a will that left my personal fortune to you if I were killed. I did that because I know you would do good with the money."

Mary was upset about what James said. She knew that she wasn't being realistic, but she didn't want to think of him being killed. What kind of God could be so cruel? Tears fell when she remembered that James had once told her that the life expectancy of a pilot was three to four weeks. James had made it through four years. When would his luck run out? When would the time come for God to take him home?

"I'm sorry," Mary said when her tears finally came under control. "I usually don't cry like that unless I'm upset. I suppose I'm upset."

James gave Mary a gentle kiss. Then he wiped her tears away. He wished he could do more to help her, but the only thing he could think to do was get out of the war alive. He loved Mary very much. But he cared for his men, too. His men had often told him that it was his leadership that was vital to them, that kept them alive.

"I'm sorry I upset you," James said. "We may not even get the order to fly that dangerous mission. I don't know why I felt the need to be realistic."

"I wish all the senselessness of this war would end," Mary said. "I've seen so many heartbreaking things since I've been working here. I don't know if I can go on with my medical career after the war is over. What is the point?"

James knew much of the difficulty Mary had in her career. He knew the pain Mary felt for being denied opportunities as a surgeon because she was a woman. She also had to put up with men like his father who believed that women had no place in the medical profession. She probably couldn't see right then that she saved more lives than she lost.

James looked at his watch and sadly realized that he had to get back. He hated to say goodbye to Mary. He truly wished that he knew what to do to help her. But then he thought the only thing he could do was love her. James was willing to do that for the rest of his life, however long that may be. He kissed Mary with all the feeling he had, which was quite a lot.

"I have to get back," he finally said to Mary. "I don't want to go yet. But I have to."

"Promise me you'll be careful and stay safe when you fly," Mary said.

"I promise with all my heart," James said. "I know I have a lot to live for."

James stood and helped Mary up. They walked to where James's car was parked. He gave Mary another deeply felt kiss. Then he got in his car and rolled down the window.

"I love you very much," he said to Mary.

"I love you very much too," Mary said. Then James started the engine and drove off.

She watched him drive away. Mary felt the tears fall again when she was gripped by the feeling that she would never see James alive again.

Not too long after James left, the field hospital Ste. Marie was overrun with casualties. Mary watched as the ambulances came to a stop. She sorted out the men with the worst injuries, so they could be treated first. It seemed like the influx of casualties would never end. But finally it did. Then Mary ran inside to prepare for surgery.

While she was getting ready to perform her first surgery, Mary felt her heart break all over again because of the horrible wounds that she had been seeing. When she was ready Mary went into the operating room. A nurse put gloves on her hands. Mary walked to the operating table and looked at the patient's wound in his thigh.

"He's under, Dr. Gordon," her assistant said.

"Thank you," Mary said.

Then Mary set to work. Her concentration and focus on what she was doing was sharp. She was determined to save this man's life if she could. As she worked, Mary said a prayer. Mary knew she had a good team working with her, which was a comfort as she did her delicate work. Finally her first operation was finished. She checked the wound and bandaged it. Mary breathed a sigh of relief that everything went well.

But she didn't have much time to think before the next patient was brought in.

Later in the night, when the influx of casualties had slowed down, Mary found that all of her operations had gone well. Amid all this pain and suffering Mary was happy and relieved at how her surgical skills were still growing even though the war was terrible. When she was able to take a moment for herself, Mary thought of James and said a prayer for him. One of her surgical cases had been a pilot. He didn't make it through his surgery, which scared Mary to death when she thought of James. She started saying another prayer for the man she loved so much. But before she could finish it and give in to her worry, another round of patients had arrived. She had to focus.

When James returned to the airdrome, he felt more tired than he ever had in a long time. He didn't understand why he had to tell Mary the reality of what his situation was as a pilot. James remembered that Mary always got upset when he talked about that. She had lost so many people that she loved—her father, mother, brother, sister-in-law, and her first husband. He would have to keep trying to see that he wasn't another loss for the woman he loved.

James was lost in thought as he made his way into the officer's mess and up to his quarters. He was so filled with regret that he obeyed his father when he forbade him to marry Mary because she was a woman doctor. His father had allowed his sister, Sara, to go to university and read law. He had allowed his mother, Susannah, to pursue her interest in aviation. What was so bloody wrong with a woman doctor? James felt upset when he still couldn't understand what his father had been thinking. When he felt too tense to sleep, James went downstairs and into the flight office. He was hoping that there was a pile of work waiting for him, so he could concentrate on that and take his mind off his frustration and pain. But there was no work to do. So James decided to go back upstairs.

James was finally alone in his quarters. He decided to take out his stationery to write to his solicitor as he had promised Milne he would do. James thought that maybe being a duke wasn't so bad if he could use his money and position to help people. He rested his hand on his forehead to think through the letter as he wrote it:

Dear Arthur—I'm writing this letter to you on behalf of one of my pilots, Lieutenant Robin Milne. He was shot down while flying a reconnaissance mission as a member of my flight. He broke his back and needs time to heal before he can care for his widowed mother. I am authorizing you to render any assistance to Lieutenant Milne that he might need to care for himself and for his mother. Money is no object. Please write to me when you receive this letter. Thank you kindly.

Captain James Allen
Royal Flying Corps and Duke of Essex

After he finished James read the letter over. When he was satisfied, James sealed it in an envelope and made sure it got into the mail. His solicitor, Arthur Henderson, was both trustworthy and discrete. James said a prayer of thanks that he was able to help Milne in this way. He knew he would do this for any of his men if they needed it. After all, they were not just brother officers to him; they were brothers.

James decided to go into the officer's mess to see what was going on and spend time with his men.

That also meant a lot to him. James heard something bawdy going on, so he wanted very much to at least listen.

He saw the new man Bryan Murray standing by the piano singing songs. Not only were the songs bawdy, but Murray was singing them in a hilarious and off-key way. As usual Sean McElroy was playing the piano in his beautiful way. James got a drink from the orderly and sat on the sofa to listen and enjoy the hilarity. He had always been glad of the camaraderie among the members of C Flight. The camaraderie was why they were so successful as a team. When the singing was over, James applauded the musicians and gave them all pats on the back.

Not too long after that, James was sitting in the flight office going through still more paperwork when Baker came in.

"You have orders, sir," Baker said as he handed James an envelope. James found that his flight had received the order he had been dreading.

"Oh, God," James said. "We have to attack the Boche reinforcements a mile or two behind their lines with low-flying aeroplanes. Call the men together after they finish their breakfast."

"Yes, sir," Baker said.

When the men gathered together, they all saw the serious expression on James's face.

"We have a difficult mission ahead of us today," James said. "We have to go a mile behind the enemy's lines and attack their reinforcements with low-flying aeroplanes. We are still on the offensive. Any questions?"

When there were none, James let his men go to eat their breakfast. He didn't feel hungry, but James also knew how hard it was to fly on an empty stomach. He went out into the mess and saw that his men were eating their usual pre-flight breakfast of hard-boiled eggs and coffee. He sat and joined them.

James noticed that little was said about the mission. He wondered if they were as worried as he was. When the time came for James and his men to go, they got into their aeroplanes without saying a word. James had noticed the streamers on his aeroplane again. He vowed that he would stay ultra-vigilant to make sure that his men came home.

During the mission, James watched closely for enemy aeroplanes. He was surprised that none were coming. That is, he was surprised until he heard fire from the ground. Reggie Spencer-Holmes, a brand-new pilot just over from Blighty, was hit. His aeroplane caught fire and fell to the ground. James flew even lower and shot at the machine gun nest that had shot down his man. He hit two of the four men in the nest then pulled up to try to avoid the fire of the remaining two men. James heard more gunfire and knew that Corky Robinson had also been shot down. So James felt that he had no choice but to call off the attack. He was angry that he didn't get another shot at the surviving members of the machine gun nest, but his aeroplane had been damaged by earlier fire. He limped home with Sean McElroy feeling angry about the losses his flight had sustained.

When James got home he went into the flight office. After he took off his gear and hung it up behind the door, he went into the officer's mess because he felt like a good stiff drink. He didn't notice that Sean McElroy was sitting at the piano until he heard the music begin. James stood by the piano and joined in singing the RFC song that Sean was playing.

During the music James was able to forget the pain of what had happened that day to Corky Robinson and Reggie Spencer-Holmes. They had both been reported missing. James felt these losses because Reggie and Corky had been the clowns of C Flight. Reggie's sense of humor had been bawdy and unique, especially because he was the son of an earl. Many times, when the pressure was intense, Reggie and Corky knew what to do to get a laugh out of everyone. James couldn't believe they were both missing. But when he sat down to dinner, the fact of the two missing men was driven home in a deeper and more painful way by the two empty chairs at the table. No one dared to sit in those chairs in memory of the missing men. No one had anything to say, so supper was quiet and subdued. The next day, James got the word that Corky Robinson had been taken prisoner by the Germans. But Reggie Spencer-Holmes was confirmed killed.

As he prepared for Reggie's funeral, it was all James could do to keep his tears at bay. In situations like this there was no such thing as the stiff upper lip. It didn't seem fair that good men like Reggie had to be killed. He was thankful that Corky Robinson had been spared and was a prisoner. He hoped that the Germans wouldn't be too hard on him. But there was no way that James could know. Yet again he had to write the dreaded condolence letter. He got out stationery and began to write.

Your Lordship—I am so sorry to inform you of the death of your son, Reginald, who we knew as Reggie. Reggie was new to our flight. But he was still a pilot of great promise and talent. He brought great warmth and humor that helped us in dark times. For that reason his loss was terrible and sad. Please pass my condolences on to your family.

Sincerely yours,
Captain James Allen
Flight Commander
Royal Flying Corps

After the funeral, James stood on the hill. The padre spoke with him. "Captain Allen, are you alright?" the padre asked.

"I don't know if I am or not, padre," James said. "I wonder when all this killing will end."

"We have no way of knowing that, Captain," the padre said.

"I keep wondering how this could be a part of God's plan," James said.

The padre looked at the two fresh graves, those of Reggie Spencer-Holmes and Steven Parker. He put his hand on James's arm and gently squeezed.

"I'm sorry that I can't help you, Captain," the padre said. "Sometimes there is no answer for the evil that men do to each other. I've been asking the same questions that you have. I also haven't got any answers."

"May I ask a favor of you, padre?" James asked.

"What is it, Captain?" the padre asked.

"Keep me in your prayers," James said. "That would help me."

"I will," the padre said.

When James got back to the flight office he sat thinking about the men he had lost. He felt no little amount of pain that he wasn't good at writing those condolence letters. He wondered how many more he would have to write before the war was over. The feelings of pain and despair over the deaths overwhelmed him. *It makes no damn sense*, James thought to himself. He got more upset as he thought about all the losses he'd had to face during the course of the war and wondered when the killing would end. Then suddenly it came to James that the killing might never end. That one feeling pierced him.

"When will my turn come to be killed?" James said out loud.

"Are you alright, sir?" Baker asked when he came in and heard James mulling aloud.

"We lost three men in three days," James said. "Steven Parker, Corky Robinson, and Reggie Spencer-Holmes. So I'm not alright."

Baker wished that he knew what he could do to help James get through his deep feelings of loss. But he was just a sergeant. James was a captain, his superior. Baker set to work on the his paperwork figuring that the best thing he could do to help James was to keep C Flight organized as best he could.

James, for his part, realized that this was exactly what Baker was doing. He paused and watched Baker do his work.

"Thank you for your help, Baker," he finally said. "Knowing that you're here to assist me takes some of that weight off my shoulders."

"Just doing my job, sir," Baker said. The two men worked together in silence.

When James was alone, his heart felt broken in the worst way possible. The only person he could think of to talk to was Mary. Sean McElroy was right in the thick of the pain with him so that's why James didn't feel he could talk to him. James took out the Royal Flying Corps stationery and a pen and wrote.

Dear Mary—I'm sorry that I didn't write to you sooner. I hate how I'm always too busy to write to you or, even better, to see you. I had to write to you because I am heart sore since I lost two more men yesterday. We lost Corky Robinson and Reggie Spencer-Holmes. Reggie was the son of the earl of Devon and heir to the earldom. He was a lot like me in that he wanted to serve his country through being a pilot. Corky was an orphan. He joined the RFC in Canada to see a bit of the world. He survived being shot down and was taken prisoner of war. The point is that Corky is not here. He and Reggie were the jesters of C Flight. They always knew what to do to make us all laugh. That's what makes the loss so difficult. I'm always sorry about writing to you about pain and fear. I hesitate to write about those feelings because I know you worry. You have been through so many terrible and tragic losses in your life. I'm trying hard not to bring more of that to you. I love you very much and don't want to bring you more pain. There is one terrible truth that I live under. It's simple. One little mistake could send me to my death. Be that as it may, I still need to talk to you, Mary. I feel so alone and lonely without you by my side. Sometimes I think about our future and the life we're going to have and our unborn children. I want that future very much. I want so much to beat the odds to have our life together. Know that I love you very much.

James

When James finished the letter, he couldn't breathe. His feelings were intense and heartbreaking. He used to think that since his father died, nothing stood in the way of his marrying Mary. But James was wrong. Something was standing in his way to marry Mary—the war.

Meanwhile, Mary truly wondered when this battle would end. When there was a small break, Mary went over to her friend Dr. Anne Palmer, put her hand on her arm, and gently squeezed.

"How are you doing?" Mary asked.

"I am fine," Anne said. "I'm glad we're having a little break, though. I've never seen such carnage in all my years as a doctor."

"I know," Mary said. "Sometimes all you can do is pray."

"I do that all the time," Anne said. "It does help."

Just then more ambulances drove up. Mary and Anne sorted out the patients so the severely injured could be treated first. Nurses came out to help them, so they got through the sorting quickly.

"I think we have to get ready for surgery," Mary said. Anne sighed and followed Mary in.

By the time the surgeries were completed, Mary was exhausted. But she knew that she wouldn't be able to sleep. She thought of James as she walked the wards checking on patients. At one point she ran into a nursing sister.

"Is everything alright?" Mary asked the sister.

"Everything is fine, Dr. Gordon," the sister said. "Thankfully all the patients are quiet."

"That's good," Mary said. "I'll leave you to it, then."

"Good night, Dr. Gordon," the sister said.

Mary went to her quarters. In the still quiet of the night, Mary couldn't help but think of James. She decided to write to him because she felt like she needed to talk to him.

My dearest James—The wards are quiet. Thankfully no new patients are coming in. In this quiet I miss you more than I can say. I hope you are well, my love, or as well as can be expected in this horrific situation we find ourselves in, this terrible war that has no end in sight. I hope you remember that I do love you very much and pray for you every day. I have to admit that I'm scared for you, especially when horribly injured pilots come into the hospital. Losing you would be the worst loss of any I've endured. Please be careful, my love. I miss you and need you. All my love.

Mary

But before she could seal the letter in an envelope, there was a knock on her door. Mary answered and was surprised to see Anne there looking distraught.

"Come in," Mary said. "Have a seat and tell me what's wrong."

"I lost a patient," Anne said. "I swear he was only twelve or thirteen years old if he was a day. I don't understand why children would want to fight in a war."

"I think they lie about their ages to enlist because they see what's going on around them," Mary said. "They get caught up in it like any man would. It's unfortunate."

"You're probably right," Anne said. "It's been very much on my mind. But I'm still sorry I bothered you with it."

"Anne, my goodness, we are friends," Mary said. "In fact you're my best friend. I miss the talks we used to have. You must never hesitate to talk to me."

"Thank you very much," Anne said.

Anne and Mary walked to the door. They hugged. Then Anne left.

Soon after that point, James was sitting in the flight office wondering when replacement pilots would join the group. There were only three men left—himself, Bryan Murray as an observer, and Sean McElroy. James wondered if the three of them would be successful in carrying out their missions.

As it turned out, James didn't have to wait long for the replacements. Two men, Lieutenants Edward Samson and Charles Baldwin, arrived within the week.

"Welcome to C Flight," James said to the two men.

"Thank you, sir," both men said at once.

"We're glad to have finally gotten an assignment," Samson said.

"Your quarters will be in this building with the other officers," James said. "Supper will be in two hours. You can join us then. You'll start on missions tomorrow."

Even as he spoke to the new pilots, James was burdened with wondering how long these men would last. He had seen too many men hurt and killed in the recent past to not wonder about Baldwin and Samson. When the mail came James found that he had received a letter from Mary. It seemed she was as heartbroken as he was because of the horrific wounds she saw on the injured men who were brought to her field hospital. James wished there was something he could do to bring this damned war to an end. He wondered about the damage being done mentally to himself and Mary by this long, drawn-out conflict. James thought he might be overdue to be sent home for a rest. But then he wondered who would lead the men if he was sent home. Because Milne was gone Sean McElroy was the most senior and experienced pilot, so he would have to be the acting flight commander. But James knew that he wouldn't get to go home soon.

He sighed and got back to work on the mess of papers that were on his desk. When he finished, James decided to go to the hangar and check his aeroplane. One never knew when an emergency would arise, so he wanted to make sure everything was ready. But before he could leave, James found an envelope from his solicitor, Arthur Henderson, mixed in with everything else on his desk. He opened it carefully and read the letter enclosed.

Your Grace—I received your letter and am replying to you as you asked. I have prepared all the paperwork to set up a fund for Lt. Milne and his mother. I put one million pounds into this fund and have the papers ready for him to sign whenever he comes home and is discharged from the hospital. I hope this meets with your approval.

Sincerely yours,
Arthur Henderson

James knew that Arthur Henderson was a good man and was pleased with his solution on what to do to help Milne. That meant one burden was taken away from him. But unfortunately James knew he had many more burdens to relieve. James slowly made his way to the hangar.

"Is something wrong, sir?" Jones asked when James came into the hangar. "I checked her myself a little while ago."

"You did nothing wrong, Jones," James said. "Before I was a pilot, I was an engineer, so checking my machine is a habit I started."

"Yes, sir," Jones said.

"Good," James replied as he finished his check and walked away. "Carry on."

Jones set back to work. James knew he had a good crew of mechanics to look after C Flight. It was just as he said. He checked his aeroplane out of habit.

When he finished his walk, James felt ready to go into the mess. He knew that Sean McElroy was out on patrol. He hoped he would get to talk further with Baldwin and Samson. It turned out that James got his wish. Baldwin and Samson were there.

"What made you want to serve in my flight?" James asked them when they were comfortable together.

"We heard of you by reputation when we were at St. Omer waiting for our assignments, sir," Baldwin said. "We heard how good you were as a pilot and how much you care about your men."

"They said you are the best flight commander in the corps, sir," Samson said.

That was news to James. He wondered why the news never found its way to where he was. It was totally maddening that it was thought he was the best flight commander in the corps when he had lost four men in such a short space of time. All that James knew was that he was a conscientious flight commander, so he concentrated on doing his job and didn't worry about anything else.

One day not too long after Baldwin and Samson arrived, James found them standing around the piano singing RFC songs with Sean McElroy playing. James was glad to see McElroy playing again. It always gladdened his heart when Sean played and sang. Sean had been reading music at Cambridge before the war started and hoped to return to his studies when the war was done. James truly hoped that McElroy would be able to return because his musical talent was beyond comparison. Many were the days that James had returned from difficult missions to find McElroy playing beautifully on the piano. James was extremely thankful that McElroy was there because his music always lifted his spirits. James walked to the piano and joined in the singing.

"There's new mail from headquarters, sir," Baker said as he handed an envelope to James when he was finished singing.

James didn't know what to make of the information he found. He knew that he had to gather the men together as soon as he could.

"Baker," James said. "Who is out on patrol right now?"

"Mr. Baldwin and Mr. Murray, sir," Baker said.

"I wish they hadn't gone out alone," James said. "I just got information that German reconnaissance aeroplanes are planning incursions into our territory."

James knew that cautious tactics and skillful stalking were extremely important and wanted to be sure that his men knew that, too. James looked out the window when he heard a aeroplane land. Thankfully Baldwin and Murray had made it back safely.

James sat at his desk. Baker followed suit and began working on what was left on his desk.

"Baker," James said. "Take a message. Tell the men that they are to fly in pairs and to be on the lookout for German reconnaissance aeroplanes. Post it on the message board as soon as you're done."

"Yes, sir," Baker said.

The next day, James and Samson were the first two pilots to go out on a mission as a pair. Bryan

Murray was flying with Samson. James didn't have an observer. Suddenly, James saw two German aeroplanes in their sector. He waggled his wings at Samson. They quickly went on the attack. At one point, James opened the throttle and overtook the German aeroplane he was chasing. James quickly got into position and gave the German aeroplane a good burst. He smiled as he watched it go down. The German observer was pulled out of the machine and fell to his death. James flew over to help Samson and Murray. But Murray shot down the other aeroplane by himself. They broke off the attack and headed for home as quickly as they could.

Mary was exhausted and devastated by what she saw through this terrible influx of patients. She still wondered when this damn war would end. Sitting in her office, she thought about James. She prayed that he was alright. Mary was extra worried because she hadn't heard from him in a long while. Mary was startled when she heard a knock on the door.

"Come in," Mary said

Mary was surprised when she saw Anne come into her office.

"Are you alright?" she asked Mary. "I've been worried about you."

"I'm just tired," Mary said. "Running this hospital is tiring. Then on top of that I have to care for patients, write papers, and write letters to James."

"You do it better than most people would," Anne said. "You're special because you care so much."

"That doesn't make things easy," Mary said.

"Do you want things to be easy?" Anne asked.

"Think of everything you're learning, of how you're growing as a surgeon."

"Of course," Mary said. "You're right. I'm glad you're here. You always help me see sense. But I would feel much better if I would hear from James. Every time a wounded pilot comes in, I wonder if it's him."

"James is a skilled and experienced pilot," Anne said. "I hope that skill and experience will help him stay alive."

"I hope so too," Mary said.

While she was talking to Anne, Mary went through the papers on her table and found a letter from James.

"I see you have an important letter," Anne said. "Do you want time alone to read it."

"You can stay," Mary said. "I'm sure the letter is short, so it won't take me long to read it."

Mary opened the letter carefully and took the one page out of the envelope. Tears filled her eyes as she read it.

Mary—I'm sorry I haven't written to you in a long time. We have been going out on long missions every day. I hope everything is well with you. I worry about you and pray for you every day. As I'm writing to you, I'm preparing for my next mission. That's why this letter to you is so short. Know that I love you very much.

James

"What's wrong?" Anne asked. "Is James alright?"

"He's fine, thank the Lord," Mary said. "They're having him and his men go out on long missions every day, so he can't write as often. I'm crying because I'm glad to hear from him."

"I'm glad you heard from him, too," Anne said.

"I can't write back right away because I go on duty in five minutes," Mary said.

"I hope I have an easy day."

"I hope so, too," Anne said.

Then Mary and Anne went outside together. Anne watched as her friend walked down the hallway toward the wards to start her day's duty. She only hoped that everything would go well for Mary. If anyone deserved to be happy, it was her. But things didn't go so well for Mary that day. There was another influx of patients. Mary was working hard with her staff to take care of the seemingly endless stream of casualties that were coming into Ste. Marie. She wasn't even sure where the battle was, just that it was a bad one. When all the casualties were sorted out as to who was most badly injured, Mary went inside to prepare for the urgent surgeries she would have to perform.

One day the men of C Flight were gathered in the office. They wondered what was going on this time.

"A stiffer challenge has arisen for us than going after German reconnaissance aeroplanes," James explained. "We have to determine whether a German attack is going to take place. We'll have to operate at 20,000 feet, so be prepared for breathing difficulties.

For the benefit of the new men, these kinds of encounters never last long because we lose height and break away. So do the Germans."

James and his men walked to their aeroplanes in silence.

Warner joined James in the aeroplane. Then Jones took James through his start-up procedure.

"Switch off. Petrol on," Jones said.

"Switch off. Petrol on," James repeated as he followed the directions.

"Air closed. Suck in," Jones said.

"Air closed. Suck in," James said.

"Contact," Jones said.

"Contact," James said.

James taxied onto the field and took off when he got up to speed.

The climb to 20,000 feet was slow and monotonous. But when he got there he soon developed breathing issues. He looked around and found that his men were following closely. Then Warner took photographs that showed the Germans were preparing for an attack. James heard singing and clicking noises in his ears. He was frightened because he couldn't hear anything. When Warner signaled he was done, James dove the aeroplane to a lower level. The rest of C Flight soon followed. James was relieved when his hearing came back. When it came time to return to their airdrome, James realized that there would be difficulty in flying against the westerly winds. He went down and picked up speed. It seemed like it took him a long time to cross the British lines, but he finally did so.

Not too long after that point, James received orders that he and his men had to go back to observation duties. The missions just kept coming.

"We have to cooperate with the artillery," James told Baldwin when he asked about the new mission. "We have to take more photographs and identify targets."

"When does the mission start, sir?" Baldwin asked.

"Tomorrow," James answered.

The next day, James and his men hovered over the German lines to direct the shells right onto their targets. Sometimes the aeroplanes stayed briefly at a fixed point in enemy territory. It was a wonder that no one got shot down.

"It was because of a strong southwest wind," McElroy said later when Baldwin told him what happened. "You throttle down to fifty miles per hour and just stay there."

"What surprised me was that they didn't fire on us," Baldwin said.

"I think the fact that they didn't fire on you was because they were being so effortlessly watched," McElroy said.

For all their work and the work of other squadrons, the British had not determined when the offensive was to begin. They just knew that it wouldn't be far off.

"Because we don't know when the offensive is to begin, we have to stay alert and prepared," James said. "It won't be easy. But I know we can handle it well."

But when James was alone in his quarters, he wasn't so sure that his men could handle this situation. That feeling on James's part wasn't because of a lack of confidence in his pilots. They were skilled men. James was worried because of the constant stress and pressure they had to face. One little mistake could send them spiraling down to their deaths. He wished he could see Mary again. She would know what to say and do to help him deal with this uncertainty. He couldn't see her now simply because he was too busy. But there was only so much that a man could stand on his own.

The next morning, the morning the attack was to begin, James woke up to the sound of heavy bombardment. He dressed quickly. He hoped that his men were not in a panic. But when James went out on the field, he saw that there was heavy fog. James hated the thought that he and his men would be blinded by this mist. His men had to be frustrated because all they could do was wait for the fog to clear.

When the fog finally cleared, James got his men up in the air as soon as he possibly could. He was wondering what the hell was going on. They called for special artillery fire on some of the enormous German targets, but none came. They even used the call for a really important target. But still there was no response. James decided that he must visit the batteries to find out what was going on. He discovered that not a single battery he visited had gotten their wireless antenna up. James knew that his most important duty was to support the artillery. But there was no artillery to be supported.

James was sitting in his office doing paperwork when Baker brought him a new envelope. He was so exhausted that he almost couldn't think straight.

"Do you know what this says?" James asked as he read the message. "We're ordered to bomb and fire at the enemy infantry and transport. Tell the men to meet me in the hangar."

"Yes, sir," Baker said

James went into the hangar. While he was waiting for the men to arrive, he sought out Jones, the mechanic.

"Jones," James said. "I want you to arm my aeroplane with four 20 lb. bombs. The rest of the men will have to carry 800 lbs. of ammunition among them."

"Understood, sir," Jones said.

As Jones left to carry out James's orders, the men began to arrive in the hangar.

"What's going on?" Sean McElroy asked.

"We've been ordered to follow the enemy infantry and attack them," James said. "I'm carrying four 20 lb. bombs. The rest of you will carry ammunition. I think you all understand the risks in this mission."

"We do, sir," the men said together

"When do we go?" Samson asked.

"As soon as the aeroplanes are ready," James replied.

It didn't take long for the aeroplanes to be ready. Warner got in his aeroplane with James. The other men followed suit. The mechanics took them through the start-up procedure. James looked around at the rest of his men. Sean McElroy was closest.

"Switch off. Petrol on," Sean's mechanic said.
"Switch off. Petrol on," Sean said.
"Air closed. Suck in," Sean's mechanic said.
"Air closed. Suck in," Sean said.
"Contact," the mechanic said.
"Contact," Sean said.

Then Sean's engine came to life. All the aeroplanes took off one by one.

James and his men followed the road until he saw the German infantry in action. Then he dove to about 500 feet and looked for a target. What James found was enemy infantry advancing on the road. He released the bombs and saw them hit in the center of the road. He heard the explosions and saw smoke. The rest of his men fired at the enemy dispersing along the road. Then James led his men to dive on the Germans in the open. When the ammunition ran out, James led his men home. But they were not finished for the day yet. They waited for their crews to rearm their aeroplanes. When that task was completed, they were all back in the air. Back at the lines they saw the enemy and the shells that were bursting everywhere. Samson spotted a German aeroplane. He was well above it, so he was able to shoot at him. Samson shot the observer because the rear gun was not firing. The German aeroplanes nose dipped. When Samson looked a second time, the German was gone.

James, for his part, was pleased with how his flight was performing. His men seemed to be keeping their composure, which helped them in the end. He gave a signal for the men to shift into low-level attacks to help the infantry and slow the Germans down. They posed problems for the German antiaircraft guns. They had gone forward as far as they could to protect their infantry from strafing. This was a life and death struggle so they had to dive in regardless of the risk.

The next day James and his men saw that the British resistance to the German advance was causing great casualties in places. That cheered James greatly even though he was tired. But he knew that the battle was in no way over. He saw enemy troops wherever he looked. He signaled for his men to shoot at them until their ammunition ran out. Soon after that C Flight found a great many more men and noticed that they were not taking precautions against their attacks. James trusted his men to make the right decisions on how to proceed. They knew that the safety of the army was their main concern and their own survival was secondary in the scheme of the battle. If they had the chance to intervene to save British troops on the ground, they must do so.

At one point during the fight, James noticed that his petrol was running low, so he made for home as quickly as he could to refuel. There were Germans on his tail, but fortunately for him they were, for the most part, missing when they fired at him. While he was waiting for his aeroplane to be refueled, James went into the flight office. He found a congratulatory memo from one of the generals. He was so tired that he didn't take notice of the name.

To Captain James Allen Flight Commander C Flight— Please accept my heartfelt congratulations to you and your flight for the superb way in which you have carried out your missions. Keep up the good work.

James struggled to read the memo because he was so tired, but he was pleased that someone was taking note of the sacrifices he and the men were making. James put it aside to read to the men.

The next mission was ground strafing. No one in C Flight liked ground strafing. Every man hated being a constant target. They hated that it was a matter of luck rather than skill as to whether or not they got shot down. They hated that it wasn't always easy to see British troops. While they were trying to decide who was who in the air, they were vulnerable. James worried that he and his men had been flying and fighting for five straight days. He knew they had to be rested, or they would be put out of action. But rest wasn't forthcoming for C Flight. The fight continued. They even had to fly in the rain. The men had to fly very low. When they looked for landmarks, the rain cut into their faces and blinded them for some seconds. The first warning many of them had that they were near the line was a dull sound that moved the aeroplane a few feet. James led his men down to 100 feet and saw what was happening a mile or so around them. They gave everything they could in the common cause of the battle.

When the battle was finally over, James and his men realized that the British had finally achieved air superiority. It had happened slowly. But the main thing was that it did happen. The RFC, which they were all a part of, had made a difference in the battle below them.

The operation was over, but James and his men were still under a lot of pressure. That was because, even though the Germans had been held back in the short term, there were still a lot of surprises that they could pull on the Allies. Pilots at the front were suffering pressure because of not only the growing casualty list but also the broken nerves of the men who remained. C Flight and the other flights in his squadron were stretched to the limit. As a matter of fact, so was he. But there was nothing he could do about that.

Or so he thought. Maybe there was something he could do after all. James had missed Mary very much. He thought of nothing but seeing her. When he had a rare day off, James went to see Mary at the Abbaye de Ste. Marie field hospital. He left Sean McElroy in command of the flight and hurriedly drove off. When he got there, Mary took James into her arms and held him tight.

"I'm so glad to see you," she said to James. "I was so scared during that battle. So many men were brought in with horrible wounds."

"I'm here, love," James said. "I made it through. It was miraculous, but I made it through."

James felt the tiredness leave his body when Mary held him close. She truly did have the healing touch. In that moment James was so thankful that Mary was a major part of his life. Suddenly a beautiful thought came to his mind.

"I have an idea," James said. "But first of all, I have to ask you a question."

Mary stepped back from James and saw a total look of love in his eyes.

"What's your question?" Mary asked.

"Will you marry me?" James asked.

"Of course, I will when the war is over," Mary said.

James took a hold of Mary's hands. She was shocked when she saw the tears in James's eyes. This could be serious.

"I don't want to wait until the end of the war to get married," he said. "You know the odds are against me. I may not make it to the end of the war. I want to know the happiness of being married to you in case anything happens to me. I have a day off today. We can go into Amiens to look for rings and find someone who can marry us. Please say yes, Mary."

"Yes," Mary said without hesitation. "I want to know happiness with you, too. So many things have been against us—your father, the war. I'm done working for the day, so let's do this."

It was James's turn to take Mary in his arms. He kissed her with great depths of feeling. When they finished with the kiss, James guided Mary to the car and helped her get in. Then he drove off as quickly as he could.

Later James and Mary were in bed together. Their hands were visible so they could both see their wedding rings. They had made love for the first time in a beautiful way.

"I'm so happy we did this," Mary said. "I'm so happy that you wanted to marry me."

"I'm happy, too," James said. "I promise you I will do everything I can to beat the odds and stay alive so we can have our life together after the war is over."

The only thing Mary could think to do was kiss James in a passionate way. They made love again and it was just as beautiful as the first time. After they were finished Mary hoped that she would get pregnant right away. That way, if something happened to James, she would still have a part of him with her.

When James got back to the airdrome, he took some time alone to consider what had happened. He and Mary had finally gotten married. Now he hoped more than ever that he would beat the odds against pilots and make it home to her. After a few moments he went downstairs to join his men.

"Are you alright, sir?" Sean McElroy asked James. "We're all worried about you because you came home and went straight upstairs."

James appreciated the concern of his men. The camaraderie among the men in his flight was important to him. It was something that he was proud of. And it was also the reason his flight was so successful.

"Actually, I am alright," James said. "I got married today in Amiens. I married Dr. Mary Gordon, the woman who is a surgeon at the Abbaye de Ste. Marie. After that last dangerous mission, I felt the need to marry her. To be honest, we don't know how long we're going to survive, so I wanted to know some happiness."

"Congratulations," McElroy said. "I wish you every happiness, sir."

McElroy went to the piano and as a wedding present played a beautiful classical piece that he knew James liked. By the time he was finished, James felt tears in his eyes.

"Thank you, Sean," he said. "As always that was beautiful."

Sean nodded.

Then he started to play RFC songs. All the other men joined in.

James sat there and listened. It pleased him to know that despite all the pressure they were under, his men were in good spirits. But he was in too serious of a mood to join in. Otherwise he would have because, even though he didn't have the best voice, James loved to sing.

While he was listening to the songs, James walked to the bar to get his brandy. When the orderly handed him his drink, James looked again at the wedding ring on his hand. The singing in the background faded for a moment as he considered what he had just done. He felt a little sad at the possibility of leaving Mary a widow again. Well, he had to get those thoughts out of his mind. Until the war ended, whenever that was, he still had many missions to accomplish. He knew that he would give everything he had to stay alive to spend a lifetime with the woman he loved.

After the singing was finished, James decided to go into the flight office to see if there was any work to be done. Another thing James prided himself on, even though he thought that the paperwork was the worst part of his job as a flight commander, was keeping up with the work, on being organized. When he sat at his desk, James saw that there was a lot of paperwork to be done. So he set to work and got through it as quickly as he could. He was relieved that the flight office sergeant, Baker, came in at one point to help him. James had to admit that he and Baker made a good team, too. Finally, when all the work was done, Baker pause and faced James.

"Congratulations on your wedding, sir," Baker said. "Mr. McElroy told me."

"Thank you, Baker," James said.

"I don't know how things are going to be different now," James said to the others as they were getting ready to go out on another mission. "We're the Royal Air Force now. I don't know how things will change for us now that the Royal Flying Corps and the Royal Naval Air Service have joined together. Maybe nothing will change. We have to carry on as best as we can. Any questions?"

There were no questions, so James and the rest of the men got ready for their next mission. James had to admit that he was scared as he suited up. To his relief, though, nothing had changed except the addition of special bombing squadrons. He wondered if the amalgamation would take some of the pressure off himself and his men. But he doubted it. It didn't take long for the men to find out that their role was helping the troops by constantly attacking the enemy on the ground. The real work was to carry on with attacks on the German troops no matter where they were.

Not too long after that point, James received word that something was happening. But he didn't know what, when, or where it would happen. It was almost too much for James. But he had to carry on his duty the best he could. He and Warner were carrying out yet another reconnaissance mission so they could finally learn what was going on.

And what James and Warner saw alarmed them. There was railway action a long way behind the German lines. There were many train timings at this station. Warner noted the presence of a German battery. James and Warner set the battery on fire. They checked on the types of guns and the layout of the battery. Something was definitely going on.

On the day the attack was planned, James looked out the window.

"How on earth are we going to be able to fly in this fog?" he asked himself.

Just then Baker came in to begin his own day's work.

"Baker, tell the mechanics to have the aeroplanes ready," James said. "I want to be prepared in case we have to fly. Have each aeroplane loaded with four 20 lb. bombs."

"Yes, sir," Baker said as he made his way out of the office.

James met his men as they came down for breakfast.

"When you're done eating, I want you to suit up and stand by your machines at the ready," James said. "If we fly today we leave the ground first. We're to drop our bombs on the advancing troops."

"Do you want me to go up and check the weather?" Sean McElroy asked.

"That might be a good idea," James said. "Finish your breakfast, then go make your check."

While McElroy was out, James waited by his machine. He was beginning to regret allowing the other pilot to go when suddenly, McElroy came in for a landing. James walked over to McElroy's aeroplane to meet him.

"It's a dud day, sir," McElroy said as he jumped out of his aeroplane. "There were clouds at 500 feet. I couldn't see the ground." Just as McElroy finished his report, Baker came out. He walked up to James in a hurry. "I have a message, sir," Baker said. "No flying today because of the fog."

Sean took off his flying helmet and threw it back in his cockpit in frustration. His tension and stress were definitely heightened. Sean then went inside while James went off to tell the other men.

When James and his men were finally able to fly, they dropped their bombs on the Germans. Then they attacked transports, which sadly, consisted of horse-drawn wagons. James and his men knew that it was necessary to kill the horses. James said prayers for himself and his men that they would survive this battle. James looked around and saw that his men were alright. The Germans had thrown a lot at them, which was worth it for the men of C Flight because they had done much damage. When they got home, James and his men were exhausted. To be honest they were surprised that they didn't make any deadly mistakes while they were in the air. They all credited James for being the man to hold them together. They understood why James was considered the best flight commander in the Royal Air Force. They also knew that they would die for James if it ever became necessary for them to do so.

When James was alone in his room, he found that he had a letter from Mary and also one from Robin Milne. James opened the letter from Mary first.

Dearest James—I am sorry that I haven't written a letter to you since before our wedding. Ste. Marie was inundated with casualties, so I didn't have time to think of anything else other than the surgeries I had to perform one after the other. I am alright even if I haven't written to you for some time. Know that I love you very much. I'm so proud and happy to be your wife. I'll pray for you when I have time to think. Please stay well and safe. Until we meet again.

Mary

Then he opened Robin Milne's letter. He was anxious to see how Robin was doing.

Dear Captain Allen—I'm sorry that I haven't written to you since I got back to Blighty. Things are going well for me. I am, quite literally, getting back on my feet. I was astonished when I went to see Mr. Henderson, your solicitor. I have no words to tell you how much the fund you had Mr. Henderson establish for us. Means a lot to my mother and me. A mere thank-you will have to suffice. Please give my regards to Mr. McElroy. Do take care, sir. All my best.

Robin Milne

James was surprised by a knock on his door. "Come in," he said.

"There's a lady here to see you, sir," McElroy said. "She said she's your wife."

"That would be Mary," James said.

"Tell her I'll be right down."

"Yes, sir," McElroy said.

James was surprised that Mary came here to meet him. Usually he went to the Abbaye de Ste.

Marie to see her and take her out. He made sure he looked presentable then went downstairs.

James found Mary waiting for him in the flight office.

"What are you doing here?" James asked. "Is everything alright?"

"I'm sorry to have come here unannounced," Mary said. "But I have news that I must tell you in person. I spoke to Sergeant Baker, and he suggested I come here."

James walked to Baker's desk and pulled out his chair for Mary to sit on. James sat at his desk. He reached across and took a hold of Mary's hands.

"So, what is your news?" James asked.

"I'm certain that I'm pregnant," Mary said.

James got scared. The last time a woman had told him she was pregnant, she later died in childbirth. Mary saw that terrified look on James's face.

"I know you're frightened, James," Mary said. "I'm going to go home and take good care of myself. I know what to do because I'm a doctor."

"I have a good staff," James said. "They know that I married you, so you must go to Essex House and let them take care of you."

"I will," Mary said.

"Would you care to have dinner with us in the mess?" James asked.

"I'd love to," Mary said. "Thank you very much."

James guided Mary out of the office and into the mess. The men all got to their feet and clapped when they saw her standing beside James.

"Let me introduce you to my brother officers," James said.

James introduced Mary to his men one by one. It touched Mary to meet them because she had heard so much about them in James's letters. She shook hands and smiled warmly at each of the men.

"I feel like I know you all from my husband's letters," Mary said. "It's wonderful to finally meet all of you."

The dinner with Mary went well. The men were as fascinated as James was by the fact that Mary was a surgeon. And Mary was fascinated by the fact that they were all pilots. James was never prouder of her than he was at that moment. He was glad to see that she got on especially well with Sean McElroy. James had hopes of staying in touch with Sean after the war to follow his progress in his studies at Cambridge and his future music career.

"Thank you so much for tonight," Mary said while they were standing outside before she left.

"I meant it when I said meeting your men was wonderful. After all, I had heard so much about them in your letters."

"They're a good group of men," James said. "I'm proud to be their flight commander. They are truly brothers to me, not just brother officers."

"I could tell that you're close to your men," Mary said. "I'm proud of you for that. I'm proud of you that you don't flaunt the fact that you're a duke."

"I never have," James said. "If I had a choice, I would turn the dukedom over to my cousin, Archie, and make a career in the Royal Air Force. Would it bother you to not be a duchess?"

"I don't think of myself as a duchess," Mary said. "I am, first and foremost Mary Allen, wife of James Allen. Then I am a surgeon. So, no, it wouldn't bother me not to be a duchess."

Just then the tender drove up. James kissed Mary goodbye and watched closely as she got in.

"I love you very much," James said.

"I love you, too," Mary said. "I promise I'll write to you."

James nodded and waved to Mary as the tender drove off. He was scared that he had said goodbye to the wife he loved so much for the last time. That was the reason he felt his heart break. He wasn't sure if he would lose Mary in childbirth or if he would be the one to be killed. Either way it wasn't a pleasant thought.

The missions didn't become any easier after he said goodbye to Mary. He began to realize how much it meant to him that Mary was nearby even though they didn't get to see each other much. He couldn't stop thinking and wondering when his luck and blessings would run out. He wondered if he would live to see his and Mary's baby born.

On the next mission James didn't do anything to change his tactics. He and Warner had flown a little too far over German lines and were caught by five German scouts and a vicious headwind to boot. James couldn't help but to wonder if his time was up, but he decided to fight as best he could and not give up. When the Germans were about 300 yards away, James decided to dive straight. Two stayed behind to forestall any help getting to James, so only three came down for the attack. When they were still too far away to fire,

James put on a sideslip and worked his rudder against it. He was moving at seventy to eighty feet per second. The rudder veiled his movement, so James fired one burst. Two of the three broke off and left one plane to continue the fight. But the enemy's gun jammed. James watched the other pilot try to remedy the jam, but he couldn't. James said a prayer of thanks but knew that he wasn't out of the woods by any stretch of the imagination. He had to do everything he could to get back over the British lines to safety. James knew he would make it home because McElroy was with him. He was the best, most experienced pilot after James himself. So, his chances were good.

"We have a new order from the commander-in-chief," James said later when he went into the mess to join his men. "We can't retreat. We have to fight on to the bitter end. I just wonder what he thinks we're doing."

"I don't know, sir," Sean McElroy said. "It's a good thing it's foggy."

"Why do you believe that?" James asked. "We're going to have to strafe the ground. We have to stop the German advance."

James and his men threw themselves into ground strafing, concentrating their efforts on stopping that German advance. The day's work turned out to be successful. More hours were flown and more bombs dropped on this day than had been done in the whole war. The German planes were also active because they were diving to kill the low-flying British pilots.

But a terrible tide had turned for James and his men. Samson and Baldwin, the two newest men, were both killed on the same day. James and Sean McElroy were the only pilots left in C Flight. Murray was the only observer. As he sat in the mess nursing his brandy, James was worried. He wondered how long it would take the replacement pilots to get there.

Fortunately, it didn't take long for the two new pilots to arrive, Timothy Woodward and Roger Barnes. They settled in well and were the experienced men James hoped he would get. The fact that he had gotten experienced men made things somewhat easier for James, which was a little bit of relief for him.

When he was in the privacy of his room, James found that he had a letter from Mary. He anxiously opened it and read what she'd written:

Dearest James—I wanted to let you know that I am home and taking good care of myself. I found out we are expecting twins. We are going to be a real family. That being said I do miss being close to you and the men. I truly enjoyed myself when I had dinner in the mess with all of you. Jenny sends you her love. She misses you very much. So do I. I'm staying at Hearthstone Manor because there is a constant fear of bombing in London. The staff has been truly wonderful. Parkes doesn't leave me alone. They are formal with me. But I still hear the staff saying that they miss you very much. They say you were always a good and fair master. I am digressing a bit, I'm afraid. I want you to know that you are missed and cared for. I love you very much.

Mary

Tears came to James's eyes when he received Mary's letter. He cried out of relief that her pregnancy was progressing well and also that he loved her and missed her very much. He was alone in his quarters, so he decided to write Mary back immediately.

Mary—I was so relieved to get your letter. I can't believe that we're going to be the parents of twins. I have to say that I hope they are both sons. We need an heir and a spare for the dukedom. It's really a nuisance. But I have to carry through with the rules. To me the gender of our children doesn't matter. I want the babies to be born healthy no matter their gender. I have to say that things aren't going well for us right now. Baldwin and Samson were both killed. I keep asking myself when this damn war will end. I so want to be home with you when the twins are born. I want them to know me as a father who loves them very much. I'm tired of all the death, pain, and horror. As I'm writing to you, I'm wondering how long the replacements Woodward and Barnes are going to last. I try hard to keep myself and my men safe. But it's getting more difficult to do. I'm sorry about what I just said. Perhaps there might be such a thing as too much honesty. I have to get ready to go on another mission. I love you very much.

James

When Mary received James's letter, she got worried. She truly wished that this damn war would end so James could be home safe with her, especially for the birth of their twins. Mary found that she still wished that she was with James so she could help him close up. But Mary had to face the fact that she wasn't that close to James. All she could do for him now was to pray.

James, in the meanwhile, was getting his men ready for the next mission. He was tired as he spoke to the men. James prayed that his fatigue wouldn't push him into making fatal mistakes in the air.

"Our next mission is to undertake an urgent reconnaissance to find out what is going on with the Germans," James said to the assembled men. "No one else seems to know what is going on, so it is up to us."

While James was on this mission, German troops were firing at him from the ground. James saw transports going along. He fired into the leading one, and a fire broke out. He was getting his bearings when he was hit with a bullet in his ankle and heel. James could feel his foot getting stiff and his boot filling with blood. It was only then that he decided to go home.

When James got back, he went straight to the dressing station. He was limping badly, so he hoped that he would be able to continue leading his men. But the medic said that he had to go to the hospital. Now the question was whether or not he should tell Mary. He was well, and on the mend, so he didn't see any need to tell her.

James only had to stay in the hospital for a week. It seemed to James as though his luck was beginning to run out. After he was released he was out on a mission. He decided to dive on an enemy aeroplane. But an antiaircraft shell burst underneath him. It hit his front petrol tank and wounded Warner in the thigh. Then the petrol caught fire. He said a prayer and hoped that Mary would remember him well. He made to jump out of the aeroplane away from the flames. He decided against it and put the machine into a sideslip. He couldn't breathe. His clothing started to burn. Then his ammunition started to go off. Enemy machines were following, still shooting at him all the time. They hit James's aeroplane. He felt pain as the aeroplane went into a spin. James tried everything he could to get the plane back under control. He managed to level out in time to hit the ground. James and Warner were thrown from the aeroplane.

James woke up in the hospital. It was Abbaye de Ste. Marie. But Mary wasn't there. He also wasn't sure where Warner was.

"I'm Dr. Anne Palmer," she told James when she saw him for the first time. "Your feet and right hand and arm received minor burns. You also had a narrow escape with your left eye. You have a cut between your eyebrow and your eyeball. Your neck is also broken. So you can't move your head. You're a lucky man."

"What about my observer, Lt. Michael Warner?" James asked.

"I'm sorry," Anne said. "He was killed by the impact with the ground.

James watched Anne with his one good eye. He knew that he was a lucky man. He knew that his injuries could have been much, much worse. But his heart was broken for Warner. They had worked well together as pilot and observer. All he could do to hold off the despair was to pray.

"Is there any way I can call Mary?" James asked a little while later. "She's going to be upset when she finds out that I'm wounded. I need to let her know that I am alright."

"You can't move right now because of your neck," Anne said. "You'll be going home when you're a little more recovered. "You'll be able to see her soon."

Now that he was badly injured and out of the picture, James couldn't wait to get home and see Mary. He wanted to be with her more than he could say. James truly believed that he was left alive to live his life with Mary.

PART TWO

LOVE

1918

But things were not going easy for Mary. It was her worst nightmare come to pass when she found out that James had been badly injured and nearly killed. He had been badly injured, and Mary was unable to be there for him and take care of him. She was devastated. That was especially true because she couldn't travel right now. Her whole inclination was to go to James. But she also knew that he would want her to stay safe and keep the babies safe. The one thing she dreaded the most was telling Jenny. As she walked to the nursery, Mary said a prayer that she would handle telling Jenny properly.

"I'd like to talk to Jenny alone, Banks," Mary said to the nanny when she got to the nursery. "Please leave us."

"Yes, your grace," Banks said as she went out. Jenny came over to Mary and put her arms around her. She wondered how she could tell the five-year-old that her daddy had been badly injured.

"Mommy, you look sad," Jenny said. "Did something happen to Daddy?"

"Yes, darling," Mary said. "He was badly hurt when his aeroplane crashed. He's in the hospital now and should come home to us soon. Let's say a prayer for Daddy so he knows that we love him and God loves him."

Jenny curled herself up in Mary's lap and said a quiet prayer for the daddy she loved very much.

While he was in hospital with time on his hands, James couldn't stop thinking about Mary and how close he had been to losing the life that he wanted with her. Even though he would have to leave the men that he cared so much about, James was still anxious to go home. He had done more than his duty. He had survived through four years of air fighting. But the horror of his flaming aeroplane did not leave his memory quickly. As he lay in his hospital bed safe and sound, James was certain that his luck had run out. He truly believed that the next time he went up in a aeroplane, he would be killed. That thought kept going around and around in his head. He couldn't build a wall between himself and such a horrible death. James remembered Robin Milne was badly wounded. He also remembered that Edward Samson, Charles Baldwin, Reggie Spencer-Holmes were all killed. So were Michael Warner and Steven Parker. Corky Robinson had been taken prisoner. He couldn't get all that out of his mind. He wanted to cry for all those men that were lost under his command. But James couldn't let himself do that because he knew that he would never stop.

Since this was the case, it meant the world to James when his men came to see him. He was especially glad to see Sean McElroy.

"Did Major Smith name you as acting flight commander?" James asked.

"Yes, sir," Sean said. "He's trying to get me promoted to captain to make it permanent."

"I wish you luck on that," James said. "I wouldn't want anyone else for my replacement. Promise me you will be careful."

"I promise, sir," was all that Sean Mc Elroy could say.

"I think I'm going to go home," James said. "I want to give you my home address so we can keep in touch. I need to know you're alright. I want to follow your music career too. You know that your music means everything to me."

"I do know that, sir," Sean said. "That means the world to me."

Sean handed James the tablet from the stand next to him. James wrote the address as well as he could without moving his head. Sean took the piece of paper and put it in his wallet.

"Thank you for that, sir," McElroy said. "I want to say now that I will miss you very much when you go home. I hope I can be as good a flight commander as you were."

"I have no doubt that you can be," James said. He reached out his hand as best he could without moving his head. Sean took a hold of James's hand and gave it a gentle shake.

"Good luck to you, sir," Sean said.

"And to you," James said.

It was hard for James to watch Sean McElroy walk away. He said a prayer that McElroy would survive the coming months. He wondered what kind of God could take such a beautiful music maker out of the world. He prayed with deep feeling that Sean's beautiful music wouldn't be silenced by a relentless enemy. That would be the most devastating blow of all for James. All he could do was close his eyes and try to rest.

But rest wasn't coming easy. He kept dreaming of his aeroplane in flames and being thrown from it when it crashed. Even though he was exhausted and in pain, James still couldn't sleep. He knew what the men of C Flight would be facing. He was well aware that the Germans had not finished their series of offensives. He knew the Allies understood that the Germans were preparing for something. James knew that his men had to fly reconnaissance missions. In previous months when he was with C Flight, two patrols that had taken off were never heard from again. When he tried to sleep, he saw British aeroplanes driven into the ground, including his own. He would wake up with a start and stay awake.

When he was awake and had time to think, James thought of Jenny and Mary. When he heard about bombing raids on London, he worried that she might be caught up in them and be hurt or killed. In the last letter James had gotten from Mary before he was wounded, she had told James that they had gone to the country house, Hearthstone Manor, so everything was fine. James was beginning to hear that so many pilots were being killed. Even though he tried not to dwell on that fact, thoughts would still intrude on his mind and he would worry.

Finally a letter from Mary caught up with James. He had his nurse open it for him because he still couldn't move his head. His heart was broken when he read it.

Dearest James—I am worried about you because I haven't heard from you in quite a while. I pray for you every day. I get scared when I read the casualty lists in case I would see your name. I fear I will see your name on the list and not be able to say goodbye. That would be the worst heartache and devastation I can imagine. Please take a few minutes out of your busy schedule to write me a short letter, so I can know that you are alright. I love you so very much.

Mary

James knew that he had made a terrible mistake in not letting Mary know what happened to him. He saw a nurse coming to check on him.

"Nurse, can you help me here a moment?" he called out. He watched as the nurse came into his room.

"What can I do for you, Captain Allen?"

"I urgently need to write a letter to my wife," James said. "She is upset and worried that she hasn't heard from me. I need to put that right."

"Certainly," the nurse said. "I think there is some paper in your drawer."

"Thank you kindly," James said as the nurse got out the paper and pen. She sat next to James with the pen at the ready. She wrote as James said these words.

Dearest Mary—I am so sorry that I haven't written to you in a long while. We had to fly many missions back to back. During one of those missions my aeroplane was hit by archie and caught fire. We crashed, needless to say. Warner was thrown from the aeroplane and killed. I suffered minor burns and a broken neck. My thought in not letting you know what happened to me was to spare you the hurt and pain from seeing me so badly injured. I was wrong in that decision. Please forgive me. I dictated this letter to one of the nurses. Because my neck is broken, I can't move my head as you know. The handwriting belongs to the nurse. I should be coming home soon. But I don't know where they will send me next. I promise I will let you know as soon as I know.

All my love,
James

"Thank you very much," he said to the nurse when she was done writing.

"You're more than welcome," she said after she wrote the address on the envelope. "I'll make sure this gets in the next mail out."

Now that he had written to Mary, James wondered exactly when he was going to go home. Anne Palmer was always checking his neck. The more he thought about Jenny and Mary, the more anxious he became to get home.

When James finally did get home, he went to Essex House and found out that Mary was still at Hearthstone Manor.

"Do you need Brady to drive you to Hearthstone Manor, your grace?" the butler asked.

"Yes, please," James said. "I still can't drive because of my wounds. If the duchess should call, please don't tell her I'm coming. I want to surprise her."

As Brady drove him down to Hearthstone Manor, James said prayers thanking God that he had survived the war as best he could.

When they arrived at Hearthstone Manor, Brady helped him out of the car then got James's things.

What James saw when he went inside was Mary reading a book, her pregnant belly in clear view. James quietly walked over to her.

"Hello, Mary," James said. "You look wonderful."

Mary turned around and looked at James. She smiled a broad and beautiful smile, went to her husband, and took him in her arms.

"This is a wonderful surprise," Mary said. "Why don't we go somewhere private and talk."

"I'd like that," James said.

As he and Mary walked around the gardens, a beautiful little girl escaped her nanny and ran up to James, "Daddy, you're home," the little girl said.

"Yes, Jenny love, Daddy's home," James said as he held her tight. "Go back to Nanny. Mommy and I need to talk."

"Okay," Jenny said when James let her go. She ran back to her nanny, and they walked off together.

"I have a surprise for you," Mary said. "I'm in the process of adopting Jenny. I thought she would at least have a mother if anything happened to you. But here you are."

"You never cease to amaze me," James said. "Elizabeth caused you so much pain."

"I was thinking of Jenny," Mary said. "She was innocent in all that mess. Not only that, she is your daughter."

Almost in spite of himself, James was a happy man. He was still upset over how he had to leave C Flight. But he had come home to a beautiful family that was soon going to grow even bigger. In a way he worried about Mary. But she knew what she was doing. He hoped that the babies would be born before he had to return to duty. He knew he had no choice but report when he was told to.

But, fortunately, before his leave was up, Mary went into labor. It was a frightening moment for James because even though he had no feelings for her, Elizabeth had died giving birth. On the other hand, Mary was a doctor.

While he waited for Mary to give birth, James saw that there was mail on the table. He doubted that he would have gotten any mail so soon. But he looked anyway. He saw letters from Sean McElroy and Robin Milne. He pulled them out and put them in his pocket.

By the time James had gone through the mail, one of the maids came to find him.

"The duchess has given birth successfully, your grace," the maid said. "She's asking for you."

At that moment, James was thankful that he had been home for the birth of the twins. He hurried to Mary's room. When James went inside, he saw her holding the twins. "We have a boy and a girl," Mary said.

James sat next to Mary on the bed. He was deeply moved as he kissed each baby on the forehead. Mary could see tears in his eyes. "Have you thought of names?" he asked.

"I thought of Matthew for the brother you lost and Susannah for your mother," Mary said.

"I like that," James said.

"I'm glad," Mary said. While James and Mary were sitting together with Matthew and Susannah, Jenny came in with her nanny.

"Hello, Mommy and Daddy," Jenny said.

"Hello, honey," Mary said. "Why don't you come to me to meet your brother and sister?"

When Jenny came close to the bed, she carefully climbed up. She gave each baby a gentle kiss.

"Go back with Banks now," James said. "Daddy will come and see you soon." Jenny went out with her nanny.

"You've made me a happy man," James said. "I feel blessed and grateful for that."

"I'm glad I was the one to do it," Mary said. "I'm thankful that we finally had our chance. I'm sorry about your father's death, but he was cruel to us in so many ways."

"Just remember that's all over, darling," James said. "We can't dwell on the past anymore."

James gave Mary a gentle kiss on the forehead. Then he took each baby from her and put them in their cradles. He went out so Mary could rest. As he had promised Jenny, James went down the hall to see her. When James opened the door to Jenny's room, he saw that she was on her bed, asleep.

"Is everything alright, your grace?" Banks asked.

"It's fine," James said. "I promised Jenny I would check on her. That's all.

"She's worn out from all the excitement," Banks said. "She was excited to know that she was going to have a new brother and sister."

"That's good," James said. "I'll leave you alone for now."

"Very good, your grace," Banks said as James turned to leave.

Later on, James was wondering what he could do with himself. He still wasn't fully recovered from his neck injury, so a return to duty, even as a flight instructor, was out of the question at that moment. He missed his men. He hoped that everything was alright, that Sean McElroy was still alright. He said a prayer for that, as always, because he didn't want McElroy's beautiful music to be silenced. He also hoped that Robin Milne was back on his feet again. Suddenly James remembered the letters he had in his pocket. He took them out and decided to read Sean McElroy's first.

Dear Captain Allen—I hope this letter finds you well on the mend. I'm writing to let you know my promotion to captain has come through. I am now the permanent flight commander of C Flight. I hope I do your faith in me justice. As I go forward as a flight commander, I'm going to follow every piece of advice you ever gave me. Please give my regards to your wife.

All the best,
Captain Sean McElroy
Flight Commander
Royal Air Force

Then James opened the letter from Robin Milne.

Hello Captain Allen—I'm sorry that I have been unable to write to you in a while. I have been talking with my father's publisher about them publishing my next book. Reach for the Sky, *the story about the pilot and his lady doctor sweetheart, has been a huge success. I will send a copy to you and Doctor Gordon as soon as I get a chance. This is an exciting time for me because my father always wanted me to follow in his footsteps as a children's book writer. I hope I will hear from you soon. Please take good care.*

Sincerely yours,
Robin Milne

P.S. My rehabilitation is finished. I can now walk with a cane.

P.P.S. Thank you for all your help to my mother and me. I couldn't have written either of my books or finished my rehabilitation without the fund you set up for us. God bless you.

James put the letters in a safe place on his desk so he could answer them once he had a chance. He prayed especially for Sean McElroy because he would be under a terrible burden as a flight commander. It seemed that Robin Milne was thriving. For that, James was grateful. He was also touched and deeply moved by the part he had played in that success. Maybe being a duke was worth it after all. Then his eye was drawn to the tube that was standing against the wall. He retrieved the tube and opened it. James took out a roll of blueprints. He carefully unrolled them and saw aeroplane designs. He had started them while he was at university but never finished them. Could he update them now? He sat down at his desk and looked them over carefully. James was surprised by a knock on his door.

"Come in," he said.

Mary opened the door. "I couldn't sleep, so I thought I would come and find you," Mary said.

"I'm glad you did," James said. "Is everything alright?"

"I wanted to spend some time with you," Mary said.

James gestured for Mary to have a seat. When she did, James held onto one of her hands as if for dear life. "I'm so thankful that you and Jenny and Matthew and Susannah are alright," he said. "I'm worried about this influenza."

"So am I," Mary said. "In a way I feel safer here in the country. But it isn't certain if it's a protection or not."

"We'll stay here for the foreseeable future," James said. "But I know there will be times when I have to go to London. I have a medical board coming up soon."

"They can't send you back to France; can they?" Mary asked.

"They could," James said. "But I think they will make me a flight instructor when the time comes."

"I hope they do," Mary said. "I know you have to go where ordered. But I couldn't bear the thought of you going back into action. I'm so worried, still, that your luck and blessings will run out."

James moved onto the sofa on which Mary was sitting. He took her into his arms and held her tight. He said a prayer that he would become a flight instructor. James couldn't bear the thought that he could hurt Mary again by making her worry if he was sent back to France. He gave her a long and heartfelt kiss. Then Mary rested her head on James's shoulder.

When it came time for James to go to his first medical board, he was still worried about going into London. It was October 1918, and influenza was still running rampant. He wasn't enamored of being in London. But he had to do his duty no matter what.

As he made his way to Essex House, James hoped the staff who remained there were safe. "Is everyone alright?" he asked the butler when he arrived.

"We are alright so far, your grace," the butler said. "It is fortunate we don't go out. We all have our duties to attend to."

"Very good," James said.

"There are letters for you on the salver by the door," the butler said. "They seem to be important."

"Would you get them for me, please?" James asked. "Then take my things up to my room."

The butler did as he was asked. James took the pile and went through it. He was happy when he saw he had gotten a letter from Robin Milne. The envelope was heavy. James retired to the sitting room to read it and see what was so heavy. James was happy when he opened the envelope and found Robin Milne's book *Reach for the Sky* and a note.

Captain Allen—I have enclosed my book for you. I hope I did well in portraying you and Dr. Gordon. I also hope that you enjoy it even though it's a children's book. Please be well.

Robin Milne

James began to read. He was pleased with the story and how it turned out. James was anxious for Mary to read it. He would have to take it home to show her.

As he made his way to the medical board, James was relieved that he had his uniform on. He saw women walking around with white feathers. They handed them to men who were not in uniform as a sign that they were cowards. Because he was in uniform, James didn't pay the women any mind. After so many years in the Royal Flying Corps and the Royal Air Force, James knew that he was the opposite of a coward. He wished that Mary was there with him. But James didn't want Mary to run the risk of getting influenza. James was glad that she was in the relative safety of the country.

After his medical board had found him unfit for duty, James wanted to see a familiar sight he and Mary had loved together. He thought of Mabel's tea shop. When he found the place, a different lady was behind the counter dressed all in black.

"Hello, your grace," the lady said.
"Do I know you?" James asked.
"I'm Elspeth, Mabel's daughter," she said.
"Is your mother alright? James asked. "Usually she is behind the counter. I would like to see her to say hello."

"She died from the flu three weeks ago, your grace," Elspeth said. "In the morning she was well. By suppertime she was gone. She insisted I keep the shop open."

"I'm so sorry," James said.

"I always loved coming here for tea."

"I know she thought the world of you, your grace," Elspeth said. "She always loved and respected you because of how down to earth you are and that you never put on airs."

James nodded. He wondered at that moment how much else in his world had changed in a bad way, first because of the war then because of influenza. It didn't seem right to him. But Elspeth broke into his thoughts.

"Would you like your usual tea, your grace?" Elspeth asked him.

"Just for one, please," James said. "My wife is still in the country."

As James waited for his tea, he felt unsettled by the fact that Mabel had died. He didn't care if it was proper or not. But James felt like he had lost a friend. That was because of how he loved her shop so much. So much had changed for James, mostly because of the war. But it had changed in other ways, too. He had lost men under his command. Even though that was the case he had still proven his mettle as a pilot by becoming an ace with thirty-one victories. He reached that milestone, and thank God, he had made it out alive. Granted it had taken a terrible injury for him to come home. But James had made it nevertheless.

Just then, Elspeth brought out the tea. James smiled in spite of his sadness when he saw the beautiful tea that Elspeth had prepared for him.

"This looks wonderful," James said. "Your mother would have been proud of you."

"Thank you, your grace," Elspeth said. But before James could say anything else, another customer came in. So, Elspeth had to take care of her. After Elspeth left, James began to partake of his tea.

When James got back to Essex House his first thought was to call Mary to let her know how his medical board went. But he decided not to because he was going back to Hearthstone Manor in the morning.

James was anxious to get back to Hearthstone Manor, to home. He needed to be around the people he loved, Mary and the children. That was the only way he could deal with the pain of Mabel's death.

When James returned home, Mary could tell that something was wrong with her husband.

"The medical board found me unfit for duty," James said when Mary asked.

"So I won't be going back to France right away."

"I thought you would be happy about that," Mary said.

"Do you remember that tea shop we used to go to in London?" James asked, cutting Mary off.

"Mabel's shop?" Mary asked. "I remember it well."

"Mabel died of influenza, Mary," James said. "I stopped at the shop after my medical board. Her daughter told me."

"I'm so sorry," Mary said. Mary sat with James and held his hands. She wondered how much more pain he could endure. She felt sad herself because she didn't know what she could do to help him.

"How are the children holding up?" James asked. "I would hate for anything to happen to them."

"So far, they're fine," Mary said. "I'm keeping a close eye on them."

"Good," James said. "Please take care of yourself, too. I wouldn't be able to bear it if I would lose you."

Mary knew what James was going through only too well. She had lost everyone she loved too.

"Why don't we go up and see the children?" Mary asked. "They would love to see you."

"Alright," James said. He stood and helped Mary. Then they went out together.

The children were sleeping when James and Mary got to the nursery. Mary checked each of the babies. She knew that infants were at risk even though she didn't want to say anything to James. Fortunately everything was fine, at least so far. James came to stand by Mary.

"They're fine," Mary said. "Banks had been doing a good job with them."

"Where is Banks?" James asked. "I thought she would be here with the children."

"She went to hospital while you were in London," Mary said. "She died as soon as she got there."

"Oh, God," James said.

"That's why I'm paying such close attention to the children," Mary said.

"I don't know what else to do. No one does."

"We're not safe anywhere; are we?" James asked.

"I'm afraid not," Mary said. Before he could get too sad, James remembered Robin Milne's book. It would be pleasant to show it to Mary.

"There was a letter from Robin Milne waiting for me at Essex House," James said. "He enclosed a copy of his book. I have it in my suitcase. I want you to see it."

James and Mary walked down the hallway to their room. James saw the book on the desk when he opened the door. He retrieved it and handed it to Mary. Mary paged through, reading the story as she went along.

"Robin told our story beautifully," Mary said when she finished reading. "I'm glad it's such a success."

"I am glad too, for Robin's sake," James said.

Not too long after that, Robin paid a surprise visit to James and Mary.

"I hope you don't mind that I came to visit unannounced," Robin said. "I missed the both of you, so I was really anxious to see you."

"We don't mind at all," Mary said. "James and I are glad to see you. Please have a seat."

James, Mary, and Robin went into the sitting room and sat on the comfortable chairs.

"Mary and I both loved the book," James said. "Congratulations on its great success."

"Thank you," Robin said. "That means a lot to me."

"Would you like to have dinner with us?" James asked. "There will be plenty of food."

"I'd like that very much," Robin said.

The dinner was congenial. James and Mary were happy to have Robin join them. In a way it was like old times for James. He remembered what it was like to sit around the mess table with Robin, Sean McElroy, and other members of his flight.

"Do you have a place to stay?" James asked. "It's too late for you to drive back to London. You can stay here. We have plenty of room."

"Thank you," Robin said. "I am tired after my drive." James rang a bell. In a few minutes the butler appeared.

"Mr. Milne is staying the night with us," James said. "Please see that a room is prepared for him."

"Yes, your grace," the butler said. Robin followed the butler out. He held onto his cane as if for dear life.

The butler saw that Robin was having difficulty. "Let me help you sir," he said.

Mary watched closely as Robin struggled to walk out. She was worried.

"I'm going to check on Robin," she said. "Something isn't right."

"Please be careful," James said.

"I will be," Mary said.

As Mary walked the hall, she stopped in her room to get her medical bag. She felt worried as
she made her way to Robin's room. Mary knocked on the door and went inside.

"I feel so hot," Robin said when Mary came in. She found him on the bed fully clothed. She took a thermometer out of her medical bag and took Robin's temperature. He had a fever. Obviously he had aches that went beyond the old injury to his back. Mary was certain that Robin had the flu. And more than likely, so did she.

"I'm so sorry," Robin said when Mary told him. "I wanted so much to see you and James that I didn't stop to think."

"I can take care of you," Mary said. "I am a doctor."

But Mary knew that there wasn't much that she could do. Outside of trying to keep him isolated, there wasn't much told do. Perhaps she could give him aspirin, but there were no other treatments available. She knew that God's will would be done. She also said prayers for Robin, that he would survive to write other beautiful children's books, and for James and the children that they would be spared. Mary wasn't quite sure if she was infected yet, so she decided to go downstairs to talk to James and let Robin rest.

"How is he?" James asked.

"He's holding his own," Mary said. "We'll have to let it take its course."

James and Mary both felt exhausted by that point. They needed to sleep, but the question was if they should sleep together.

"I don't think we should," Mary said to James when she went into their room to get a nightgown "Being close together can spread the disease."

Sadly, then, Mary took her nightgown and went to her own room. She sat on her bed and cried. Mary was realizing, under the guise of this terrible disease, how deep her love for James ran. Even though it took a horrible injury for James to survive the war, the fact remained that he had survived. She couldn't bear to think of her husband dying of this insidious disease. So sacrifices had to be made to protect the people she loved. She would have the rest of her life to sleep closely to James if they made it through this pandemic.

The next few days were anxious for James and Mary as they waited to see what happened. Robin was holding his own against the flu thanks to the aspirin Mary was giving him. Mary, herself, showed no symptoms. But James still prayed that she would be alright. It turned out, though, that Mary wasn't alright.

She realized that she was coming down with the flu herself. Why was this happening? Who would care for James and the children? She knew there was staff. But she liked to care for her family herself as much as she could. She didn't know how the children were in the first place.

James wondered what was going on with Mary. He wondered why she didn't come to talk to him as much as she usually did. He decided to go up and see what was going on. James knew for certain that he would risk coming down with the deadly flu to see Mary, whom he loved very much. Every day he flew with C Flight, he risked death and that was for something abstract, king and country. Mary was real to him, as was the great love he felt for her.

When he got upstairs, James went straight to Mary's room. He found Mary in her bed resting.

"I have the flu." Mary said. James didn't back away. He stayed as close as he could even though he knew close contact could spread the disease.

"I needed to know how you are," James said. "I suppose I found out."

A deep pain came over James when he considered the predicament that Mary was in. He had the feeling that he was going to lose her. He knew it for certain because people were dying of this flu. James saw that Mary had gone to sleep, so he covered her with the blanket that was on the bed. Then he went out. It was during this uncertain time that James began to miss flying. He knew it was the beginning of November, so he didn't have long to wait for his next medical board. He hoped he would be found to be fit to fly. Although he knew that his problems and sadness would be waiting for him on the ground when he came home, James also knew that he could enjoy the freedom of flying, at least for a couple hours.

But James didn't have that luxury at that moment. He had to stay home and worry too much. He decided to go into his study and look at his blueprints again. But James soon put them away because he couldn't concentrate. He wanted to see Mary.

Mary was awake and sitting up when James came in to talk to her.

"You should be careful," Mary said. "I don't want you to get this."

"I had to see you," James said. "I needed to know you're getting better."

"I feel a little better," Mary said. "The rest is good for me."

"I want to check on Robin, too," James said "I hope he's doing well," Mary said.

"I do, too," James said.

James went to Robin's room and found that Robin was sleeping. James was glad that he was holding his own. He decided not to disturb his friend and went to his own room to get ready for bed. But James didn't rest easy because Mary wasn't by his side. He kept fighting the horrible fear that he was going to lose her. James wondered how God could do such a cruel thing to him. He and Mary had overcome so many obstacles to be together. Then the flu had to happen. James knew that he needed to rest, so it didn't take him long to change into his pajamas and get into bed.

It also didn't take long for James's next medical board to happen. James made his way back to London feeling subdued. He was surprised to hear talk of an armistice as he walked the halls of the building where his medical board was to happen. He wondered if that could be true. James pulled a young lieutenant aside to ask what was going on.

"There is talk of an armistice, sir," he said. "In fact it should have been signed earlier this morning in France. It goes into effect at eleven o'clock."

"Thank you," James said. "Carry on."

James watched as the young officer made his way down the hallway. He found his way to the exam room and sat by the door waiting his turn. By the time James was finished, he heard Big Ben chiming the hour and the sound of a roaring crowd. He knew that it was eleven o'clock by that sound, that the armistice had taken effect. James had been found fit to fly by this medical board. But he wondered what his future was going to be now that the war was over. He decided to make his way back to Essex House so he could at least call Mary to ask for her advice. What should he do if he were offered the chance to accept a permanent commission?

"What is all the commotion, your grace?" the butler asked James when he came in.

"The war is finally over," James said as the butler took his coat and hat. "The armistice was signed earlier this morning, so people are celebrating."

"God be praised," the butler said. "How did your medical board go?"

"I was found fit to fly," James said. "But I don't know what my future is going to be because of the armistice."

At one point James had heard talk of him going to Gosport to train as a flying instructor. But he imagined that it wasn't for certain now. James also realized that he had to stay in London until he received orders. He called Hearthstone Manor.

"Hearthstone Manor" Mary said over the phone.

"It's James, Mary," he said.

"I wanted to let you know what happened with my medical board."

"What did happen?" Mary asked. "I've been wondering."

"They found me fit to fly," James said. "I'm waiting to see what my orders will be because of the armistice."

"At least they won't have to send you back to France," Mary said.

"Thank God the war is finally over. There was talk of me being a flight instructor, but I don't know what will happen with that now," James said. "I have to stay in London until I see what's going on."

"Robin recovered from the flu and went home," Mary said. "I hired a new nanny, Abigail May, for the children, so she keeps them occupied."

"How are you?" James asked. "I've been worried about you since I left."

"I'm fully recovered," Mary said. "Would you like me to come to London to keep you company?"

"I'd like that very much," James said. "It's lonely here without you."

"I'll let you know when I'm coming," Mary said. "I love you."

"I love you, too," James said.

After he hung up, James said a silent prayer of thanks that Mary had survived the flu. They were going to have their life together after all. At least that part of his future was settled.

As it turned out, James didn't have to wait long to have the other part of his future settled—to find out what his future with the Royal Air Force would be. He had been demobilized. It was time for him to be the duke of Essex after all.

EPILOGUE

1964

Susannah was satisfied with her finished manuscript for *Love and Valor*. She couldn't believe that she actually finished the book. Her agent would be pleased. She had written other books in the past as part of her life as a history tutor at Newnham College, Cambridge University. But this one held more meaning for her because it was about the parents she loved so much. Susannah was so lost in thought that she was startled by the knock on her door.

"Come in," she said.

Susannah was surprised when her husband, Anthony, came into the study.

"I thought you would still be out at the airfield," she said.

"Everything is finished," Anthony said. "'Mary's Spirit' is ready to fly, but we need a pilot. Are you free?"

"I'd love to fly her," Susannah said. "I found Father's flying coat, goggles, scarf, and helmet in the attic. I'll wear them. He always wanted me to have them. I just don't know what to do about Jenny. I promised I'd let her fly with me."

"Didn't Father have extra gear?" Anthony asked.

Susannah thought for a moment. "I remember an extra pair of goggles,"

"Susannah said. "I won't go that high on the first flight, so I think the goggles will do."

Just then there was another knock on the door.

"Come in," Susannah said.

Jenny poked her head in.

"Can I come in?" she asked.

"Oh certainly," Susannah said. "We were just talking about you."

"You were?" Jenny asked.

"Father's aeroplane is ready to fly," Anthony said. "Do you still want your ride?"

"Yes I do," Jenny said. "I found an extra pair of goggles when I was going through the attic. I have them in my room. I'll go get them."

"That's good," Susannah said.

Anthony and Susannah sat together to wait for Jenny to come back with the goggles. Anthony took hold of Susannah's hand.

"I forgot to ask you how you're doing with *Love and Valor*," Anthony said. "I'm sorry."

Susannah put the manuscript on the desk. "It's finished and edited by me," she said. "It's alright that you forgot. I know restoring 'Mary's Spirit' and making her flyable again meant a lot to you. Let me go upstairs and get my gear. Then we can go out to the airfield together along with Jenny."

Jenny returned to the study from a different direction with her goggles. She sat in the study with Anthony waiting for her sister to return.

"I'm getting more excited for my ride as the time comes closer," Jenny said. "I'm beginning to wish that I had gotten my pilot's license like everyone else in the family."

Anthony took hold of Jenny's hand. "It's never too late," he said. "See if you like flying on your ride with Susannah. Then, if you do, get your license. You can always make time to fly."

"I think you're right," Jenny said. "That's the way I can honor Mother and Father."

"I know they would have loved you to get your license," Anthony said. "Give yourself time to think about what I said."

"I will," Jenny said.

While she was alone in her and Anthony's room, Susannah felt calm and peaceful as she found James's flying gear and put it on. She looked around, as if she was expecting James to walk through the door and hug her like he always did. She walked back out to go to the airfield with her husband and sister.

When they arrived Susannah and Jenny walked into the shed and saw 'Mary's Spirit' for the first time since she was restored. She looked beautiful. When she walked around the aeroplane in her father's gear, Susannah closed her eyes and thought of how handsome and dashing he was when he was wearing this gear himself. Jenny smiled when she ran her hand over the fabric.

"I love you, Father," Susannah whispered. "I hope I do you proud."

Jenny put her hand on Susannah's arm and squeezed.

"You will do Father proud," she said to Susannah. "He was always proud of everything we did." Susannah nodded to her sister.

"Hello, Susannah," Barry Thomas of the Royal Air Force Museum said to her. "Since 'Mary's Spirit' is your father's aeroplane, I thought you should do the honors and take her on her first flight."

"Thank you, Barry," Susannah said. "That means a lot to me. I'd like to introduce my sister Jenny to Barry Thomas. He's been advising us while we restored 'Mary's Spirit.' It's a two-seater, so Jenny is going for a joy ride with me."

"It's your aeroplane," Barry said.

Susannah climbed into the cockpit and made ready for Barry to take her through the start-up procedure. Jenny climbed into the rear cockpit and strapped herself in.

"Contact," Barry finally said.

"Contact," Susannah repeated.

The engine started on the first try. Susannah taxied 'Mary's Spirit' down the field and took off. As Susannah flew her father's aeroplane, she felt his presence all around her, which made everything in the world seem right to her. Because of that, Susannah felt happier than she had since her parents had died. Jenny was truly enjoying the flight, too. She felt the same way that Mary did when James took her up for the first time. Jenny thought that James and Mary would be proud of her for going on this ride. Jenny definitely knew she would get her pilot's license. There was no doubt in her mind that Anthony was right when he said that it was never too late.

Jenny let out a roller-coaster-style scream when Susannah did all the aerobatics that James had taught her. She flew 'Mary's Spirit' as her father would have done. Now Susannah and Jenny both understood why he loved to fly so much. Susannah didn't know how long she and Jenny had been up, but she finally noticed that her fuel was getting low, so she reluctantly came in for a landing. When 'Mary's Spirit' came to a stop, Susannah took off her helmet and goggles. She had to pause and catch her breath while her excitement wore off. She gave Jenny a big hug to calm her down. In that moment Susannah was glad she had kept up her pilot's license even though she didn't have a lot of time to fly. She was busy with her work as a history tutor at Newnham College, Cambridge University. When Anthony came running up to her aeroplane, Susannah got out of the cockpit and ran toward him. Anthony picked her up and spun her around. Barry walked over to the happy couple and shook their hands.

"Well done, Susannah and Jenny," Barry said. "I'm sure your father would have been proud of both of you."

"Thank you," Susannah said. "While I was flying 'Mary's Spirit,' I was wondering if there was something we could do with her. Part of my work as a historian is studying aviation."

Anthony held Susannah close as she was talking. He hadn't seen her so happy or excited since before her parents died. He hoped that something could be worked out. Then he gave Jenny a hug, too.

"I don't know of anything educational that you could do," Barry said. "But there are air shows that you could fly 'Mary's Spirit' in. Then you could talk about your father and how he was a pioneer designer and pilot."

"That's a wonderful idea," Susannah said. "After I see about getting *Love and Valor* published, can I get back to you to talk more about it?"

"Of course," Barry said. "I'd love to. You know where I am."

"Yes," Susannah said.

Later, back at Hearthstone Manor, Susannah looked through old photographs of her parents to see if she could find one of James in his flying gear. When she found one, Susannah ran her fingers over it. She had to show this to Jenny, too. Jenny was in ground school now for her pilot's license. Susannah thought she would find the picture interesting. Then Susannah put the picture on her writing desk where she could see it.

Suddenly, she heard the knock on the door of the study.

"Come in," Susannah said.

"Forgive the intrusion, my lady," the butler said. "But this letter came for you. I thought you might want to see it right away."

"Thank you," Susannah said. "That will be all."

Susannah waited until the butler had left. Then she opened the letter. As it turned out, Beardsley and Jenkins, her old publisher, was going to publish *Love and Valor* too. Things were looking bright after all.

www.ingramcontent.com/pod-product-compliance
Ingram Content Group UK Ltd.
Pitfield, Milton Keynes, MK11 3LW, UK
UKHW022224230426
12048UKWH00016BA/1041